Chardonnay noticed Heath standing before him like a gangly tree struggling to understand whatever had happened to its fallen leaves.

"Clan Melaleuca," Chardonnay said, as if sharing a secret.

"Clan Amaryllis," Heath replied, as if confessing a lie.

"I am found out."

"You wanted to be found."

The Urban Goatherds

Also by Keith D. Jones

Merriweather's Guide to the
English Language
(2019)

Tourist Hunter
(2016)

Pyrrhic Kingdom
(2013)

The Etymology of Fire
(2004)

The Faire Folk of Gideon: Pin the
Tail on the Donkey
(2001)

The Magic Flute
(1999)

Additional information available
at the author's website

stormsdream.com

The URBAN GOATHERDS

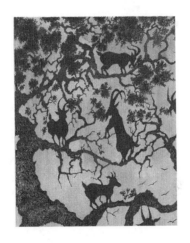

keith d. jones

Layout & Design
Keith D. Jones

Artwork
Samantha Jayewardene

ISBN
979-8-3591559-5-3

Build
(pb).2.23.2.25

Dedicated to Alice Fraser, *The Last Post* podcast, and the collected works of self-published supernatural romance novelist D'Ancey LaGuarde.

Acknowledgments

Thanks to Chris Dumas for editing the manuscript. Humorous romance is way outside my wheelhouse. The editorial advice, recommendations, and assistance were greatly appreciated.

And a very special—why am I putting this second?—thanks to Samantha Jayewardene for all the wonderful illustrations.

The Urban Goatherds

Introductions

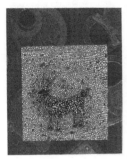

The house was on fire. It was the first thing Heath noticed, rounding the corner, driving the wagon. Fire wasn't even a surprise. He had noticed the smoke from way back and then the people running around as he had gotten closer, so the flaming house was to be expected. The surprise would have been if nothing had been burning.

Heath was merely disappointed, trying not to show it, but a sigh of quiet resignation escaped him anyway. Peregrine, riding shotgun, hearing him, voiced her own deeply felt, commiserative, and fatalistically world-weary sigh.

"That's not our fault, right?" Peregrine said, the sigh having left her unfulfilled. Heath gave her half a look. "We can't be blamed for that," she argued, pointing.

He didn't answer, just pressed the wagon forward, hoping to get past the scurrying crowds without running anyone over, the people multiplying out of nowhere, fire drawing them like flies to a cow pie. The firefighters would follow eventually.

Heath and Peregrine were forever friends, having grown up together, having known each other longer than either could remember. They were Clan Melaleuca goatherds, working the flaming-pellet wagons, a good team. Peregrine was better with people, which came in handy as they made their deliveries. The wagon—as it was affectionately called—was a diesel/elec-

tric hybrid that looked more like an armored car than
a delivery van.

Not all goatherds worked directly with the
fire-breathing goats of death that were the driving
force behind Clan Melaleuca's existence. Some goatherds—Heath and Peregrine, for example—had to
care for the dung.

The flaming pellets—as the goat dung was called—
were difficult to work with at the best of times. The
fire-breathing goats of death didn't do anything by
half measure, and that included their droppings. The
flaming pellets were volatile, dangerous, and gave off
heat lasting hours, even days with the proper care.
Enough pellets in a heap would spontaneously burst
into flame.

Cheaper than coal, safer than gas, the goat dung
was a surprisingly clean energy source, considering
where it came from. Downside was the pellets would
occasionally explode. Natural gas would, too, but flam-
ing-dung explosions were easier to contain, as Heath
and Peregrine could tell through simple observation
of the neighborhood surrounding the brightly burning
building.

The conflagration was contained to the one
house. There were frantic people—household staff,
groundskeepers—with buckets, garden hoses, and
water. The swarming masses beyond the walls were
mostly gawking and swirling around without much
apparent interest in assisting the desperate staff. Firefighters would come. The people knew they would—
eventually—so it was mostly an exciting show of billowing smoke and towering flame as far as the crowds
were concerned.

It was a nice house. It was a good neighborhood.
Street was paved with white stone. Well-manicured
trees shaded the panicking pedestrians. Each house—

majestically elaborate in design—was nestled at the center of its own private garden, surrounded by fences of gray brick and white stone.

The fire wasn't Heath and Peregrine's problem. While they were doing the rounds, making deliveries in the area, the street with the flagrantly enraged building and flailing people wasn't their block. They didn't want to get involved. It was bad for the schedule.

That didn't stop the people from waving arms at them, trying to stop the flaming-pellet wagon's progress. It was the audience-participation part of the show, and the crowd loved to participate. Peregrine leaned halfway out of the shotgun seat, opening the door, letting it swing wide for a better vantage.

"That's not on us," she hollered at the people, pointing dramatically at the burning building. "We didn't cause that."

"That's not exactly their point," Heath said.

"What?" Peregrine swung around as if she might stand on the running board and lean back into the cab to confront him.

"They want us to help."

"Well, how do they expect us to help?" Leaned back out the open door. "How do you expect us to help?"

Heath pressed the wagon forward, people slowly giving way. Peregrine slid back into her seat, secured the door. Nobody had answered. She hadn't expected answers.

"Suppose they have a point," Heath said, watching the people so that he wouldn't inconvenience too many of them.

"How you figure?" Peregrine sounded dubious.

"Flaming-pellet wagon, goatherd clan clearly marked on the side," gesturing as if to indicate points of interest on the wagon. "Should have fire-control and suppression measures."

"We've got a bucket of sand, if that's what you mean."

"Just following their reasoning."

"They can follow their reasoning right off a cliff," said while glaring at the crowd, turned, glared at Heath. "Don't follow them off a cliff."

They escaped with a minimum of bodily injuries to the gawkers and assorted random spectators who had gathered at the first flickering sign of fire. It was a wonder people didn't follow the flaming-pellet wagon everywhere, hoping for explosive death and devastation to flow in the wagon's wake.

Heath and Peregrine reached their scheduled block. It wasn't far from the fire. Clouds of dense smoke, accompanied by that inescapable burnt charcoal smell, smeared the sky. People were nervous, watching the smoke, checking the wind, but otherwise relieved that the wagon was making its rounds.

"Mister Wintershine," Peregrine said, leaning out the window at their first delivery, speaking to the young man opening the gate for them. "Did the footwork impress at the fortnight feast? Did sunshine notice—her name—April?"

The young man, Wintershine, blushed as he held the gate for them.

"I take that as promising."

Heath settled the wagon. Peregrine really was good with people, remembered everything. Heath went round to the wagon's side, ignored the words brightly painted there: *Clan Melaleuca, Marvelous and Refined Flaming Pellets, Warms the Heart and Home.* Opening the panel revealed rows of hotboxes. Each one contained a carefully cultivated and packaged heap of incendiary fire-breathing-goat dung.

"It looks like their containment shed got away from them," Peregrine was telling Wintershine as she joined

Heath, helping him remove a hotbox. "Nothing to worry about."

"That's good." Wintershine sounded relieved.

"The house is a loss," Heath said.

"Well, yeah, there is that." Peregrine balanced her end of the hotbox.

They used long poles run through hooks and rings on the sides so that the hotbox could be suspended in the air between them. It wasn't good to touch the hotbox itself any longer than absolutely necessary. They made their way to the custodial end of the house, Wintershine trailing along. He looked nervous and unsure of their efforts. A slight but noticeable increase in smoke meandering overhead had affected his mood.

"Just respect the flaming pellets," Heath said in an attempt to settle Wintershine's quiet concerns as well as draw his attention away from the sky.

The containment shed was red brick, settled at the edge of the custodial wing, and mostly underground. There were two gates that could be flipped open. One contained the nearly spent hotbox. The other gate was empty. Wintershine unlocked the empty gate. Heath and Peregrine maneuvered the fresh hotbox into it. The very nearly empty hotbox occupying the other gate was easy to remove. With the flaming pellets burned away, there were hardly any remnants, maybe some ash.

The spent hotbox was added to the racks in the side of the flaming-pellet wagon. The panel was closed, and they returned to the cab. Heath fired up the wagon and began to maneuver back out the drive. Wintershine held the gate.

"Practice that footwork," Peregrine said, leaning out the shotgun door, waving to him. She settled back into her seat for the very short drive to their next delivery.

"You have a way with people," said without looking at Heath.

"Yeah," more of a whispered sigh than words. "Why I drag you along."

"Interpersonal translator," she said. "I should print business cards."

Heath stopped the wagon at the next gate. They waited.

"Looks like Trace Davidson with the egress," Peregrine said, leaning forward, looking out the window. "Why is it always the young men with the door duty?" muttering half to herself. "Trace has a mother, three sisters, one engaged, I think."

"Expect me to remember all that?" Heath said. Peregrine's misuse of "egress" was quietly ignored.

"Give it a try," said while working the door. She leaned out the shotgun seat, shouted to the young man.

Otherwise, the delivery went well. The hotboxes were exchanged. The billowing smoke was commented upon, and Peregrine managed not to scold when Heath spoke.

"This next one is Anthony White," Peregrine said as the young man approached. "He wants to propose to his beloved, but you know," waving toward the house, "he would have to give notice."

"George must not be feeling well," she said at the delivery after as they waited for the gate, watching a young man approach. "Looks like Peter Zachery—are you even listening?"

It was several deliveries later, Peregrine looking sullen, when a house—far too close for comfort—exploded. Flames roared like fireworks reaching for the sky. Red and white bricks hurtled by overhead. Heath and Peregrine almost dropped the fresh hotbox they were carrying.

"Whoa," Peregrine said. Dropping the box would have been very bad. They practiced, balancing boxes filled with rocks while helpful friends and relations pelted them with garbage. It worked.

"Back," Heath said, and they hustled the hotbox back to the flaming-pellet wagon, dodging airborne debris as they went. "Containment shed blew."

"You think?"

They watched the flames spiral and rise like a quick-growing flower. Hunks of rock splattered the ground, dropping like miniature meteorites that had grown bored with the nighttime sky. The flaming-pellet wagon was slight shelter, but they knew it would survive. Wagon was sturdy for just such emergencies. Finally, seconds having felt like hours, the thumping of broken fragments and shattered pieces of containment shed wound down.

The fire had taken an interest in eating its way through the unexploded parts of the house rather than continue in its desperate interest in breaching the sky. People were gathering, as they always did. Peregrine stepped away from the relative shelter of the wagon, watching the show, admiring the quick multiplication of the people, and then she gave Heath a look.

"So, we're done with this block," she started to say, and then froze, eyes going wide.

She had heard it—they had both heard it—the bleating of an annoyed goat.

"How?" Heath said, barely a word, and then they were running toward the burning building.

The people, having gathered so quickly for the show, were already starting to run the other way, tripping over each other in their haste to be as far from the sound of a fire-breathing goat of death as humanly possible. It made reaching the burning remains more interesting than Heath and Peregrine would have preferred. They stopped at the property line, leaning against the well-sculpted white stone wall, looking to the swirling flames. There was more bleating from out of the fireworks show.

"What are we doing? What are we doing?" Peregrine said to nobody.

Everybody was running—spectators, friends, family, household staff, groundskeepers. The fire emanating from the ruins of the containment shed was still something of a show that very few wanted to admire. Heath and Peregrine continued to watch, hypnotized. The swirling flames parted rather dramatically, like quickly drawn curtains, and there it was, the goat.

Face was a chiseled horror show, complete with a scruff of beard, twitchy ears, stubby little horns, and eyes out of a demon's hastily suppressed nightmare. Fur was dark brown and black in mocking imitation of smoke. Goat was barely a foot tall.

It pranced forward on stumpy little legs, the ground smoldering under each hoof, wiggled its tail. The goat called out, bleating, sounding more befuddled and annoyed than angry. It seemed oblivious to the flaming hellscape around and behind it.

"It's a kid," Heath whispered, awestruck, and then seemed to take an interest in exploring his coat and trousers as if he had forgotten something.

"That's not an improvement," Peregrine said. "What are we—" turning, noticing Heath's frantic search. "You didn't."

"Back at the wagon," turning, running.

"No," Peregrine following after, trying to catch him. "This is not a good idea."

Heath reached the flaming-pellet wagon, fumbled the door open, began rummaging around in the cabin. Peregrine stood by the door, agitated, as if she might stamp her foot at any moment, flames spreading to more of the burning house behind them.

"Where? Where? Where?" Heath said. The cabin was a mess, as if random debris strewn about was a requirement of the job, nothing ever thrown out. He sorted among piles of paper, crushed coffee cups, wax-paper bags that had previously held donuts and french fries.

"Not a good idea." Peregrine watched little ketchup packets fly. "Not good," turning back toward the source of smoke and fire.

The goat was still in the devastated yard, ignoring the conflagration madly consuming the house as if it had already forgotten about the fire, or rampaging flames were simply part of its natural habitat. It called out, bleating, as if wondering why there were no other fire-breathing goats at hand.

"Got it," Heath cried, triumphant, holding aloft a set of reed pipes. The pipes were carved bone, bound together like a pan flute.

"Heathcliff," Peregrine said, watching him half-climb, half-fall from the cab.

"No fear," he said, and then was running back toward the burning house.

"It's not frightened—hey," Peregrine said, turning, running after him. "It's not—it's angry," skidding to a stop in the middle of the road.

Heath had reached the white stone fence, trembling, fumbling with the reed pipes. The goats lived on fear. They feasted on terror.

"No fear," Heath mumbled, staring at white stone, not wanting to look over the wall into the garden. "No fear."

The reed pipes—also called reeds—were the only thing that could control the fire-breathing goats of death. The goatherds practiced. They rehearsed and they trained, the work of years. A flatulent note meant a fiery death.

Heath knew the fingering. He had felt the heat in his face. The flames had singed his eyes. The goats had bleated as if mocking, teasing him with immolation. The trainers had laughed.

Heath put the reeds to his lips, tried to find a note, and lifted his gaze from the stone wall. The breath died in his throat. The note didn't stand a chance.

The goat wasn't even doing anything, just wandering slowly this way and that as if it didn't really want to leave the sumptuous gardens and enclosed yard. It called out, bleating, as if hoping for a reply. It was young, only a kid. It was lost, and it was only a matter of time before it became agitated. Then the fire would grow.

Breathing deep, knowing the goats fed on uncertainty and fear, Heath closed his eyes and sounded a note. He attempted a tune—warm, peaceful and inviting. His mother had taught him. The sound wavered but grew. She was a great teacher. He remembered that control of breath was deep in the lungs, pit of the stomach, and then he opened his eyes.

The young goat was looking at him, watching him with wild eyes of madness and despair. An ear twitched. Heath let the song grow, looking to the goat, hoping for quiet acceptance. There was none. Flames took the world, spiraling into the sky, the fire growing and growing. The trees around him burst into flame. The heat was tremendous. The stone wall shimmered and smoked. He could hear Peregrine call his name.

Heath fell back as the white stone wall became so hot it burned. He almost dropped the reeds. Stumbling into the street, unable to look away, he watched the lawn transform into a shimmering ocean of flame. The neighboring houses were lost, smoke shrouding them, fire claiming them.

Peregrine had a grip on his arm, pulling him away from the inferno. Heath continued to stumble, refusing to turn, holding the reed pipes in his hands.

"Come on," she may have said.

A car screeched to a stop, having to swerve to avoid them, and almost crashed into the smoldering stone wall. The words *Clan Melaleuca, Goatherds,* were emblazoned on the side. Men poured out, wearing long coats, hoods, and masks. They could be mistaken for firemen at a glance.

They approached the wall, swarming through the half-melted gate, and closed on the enraged goat. The reed pipe music began. Heath could hear it. The sound was unmistakable, pure, and refined. Three—four—of the goatherds surrounded the goat, playing reed pipes despite the flames.

The firestorm faltered, uncertain. The goat seemed to be considering the merits of the tune. It called out, bleating, but less concerned about an answer. The goatherds played on as if trying to find their own reply to the call.

The fire-breathing goat of death allowed the rampaging fire consuming the garden to wither and die. The house still burned, goat caring not at all about previously established flames. The neighbors would have to tend to their own houses and homes, or hope the firefighters arrived soon.

The goatherds had gotten a chain around the goat's neck. It seemed not to mind and followed willingly after them to the car. It was only a young goat, after all, and the world seemed suddenly familiar and serene again.

Heath and Peregrine watched from the middle of the road as if shell shocked while the goat trotted peacefully to the car. One of the goatherds continued to play, leaning against the fender, entertaining the little rogue engine of chaos and destruction. The goat wagged its tail.

Heath felt the reed pipes in his hands, fingers moving over the stops in time with the rhythm and the tune, and then it slowly penetrated his consciousness that he was being watched. Peregrine seemed to have the same realization. One of the goatherds was studying them, waiting until they noticed, and then he pulled his hood back, removed his mask. It was Marshall November, reed master and clan leader. Heath forgot how to breathe.

Marshall November said nothing, studying them, as if words were an unnecessary luxury and meaning could be conveyed through silence alone. Beyond him, as if anything existed past the clan leader, one of the goatherds was speaking, voice drifting absently toward them. Goatherd was using the car's shortwave radio, leaning across the front seat, reporting the rogue animal, arranging transport for it. The music, keeping the goat quiet, continued to drift and sway. The young fire-breathing goat of death seemed content.

"Don't you have a schedule to keep?" Marshall November said.

Heath felt the world give way, his blood and bones slipping through a hole in the earth, leaving nothing but a husk of skin and hair to stand beneath the sun. The reed pipes dangling between his fingers were the only thing he could feel.

"Yes, we do," Peregrine said, touching Heath's arm, pulling him away from the still-burning houses and homes.

They reached the flaming-pellet wagon, Peregrine taking the driver's side, Heath climbing into the shotgun seat without a word. Peregrine fired up the wagon. They listened to the engine grumble and groan.

"This block is done," Peregrine said as a fire engine roared into view. They drove away.

Desires

Clan Melaleuca had a farming complex on the waterfront, away from most other industries and even farther away from the more residential or urbanized parts of town. The fire-breathing goats of death that were the primary obsession of Clan Melaleuca were housed in sprawling high-walled paddocks open to the sky. The steel and concrete walls were designed to channel the occasional burst of flame or fiery explosion away from the surrounding buildings, and the heat-resistant qualities of the enclosures were enough to challenge even the most ornery or determined goat.

Water towers stood everywhere. Highly stylized and brightly painted, they resembled silent sentinels standing eternal guard over the complex, watching for fires that might spread beyond the paddock walls. Grain silos and storage buildings rested in the shadow of the towers, and beyond sprawled the clan's large communal farm houses, looking very much like slope-roofed barns sporting windows, chimneys, and doors far too numerous to count.

Out of the swirling assortment of structures that made up the farming complex, the flaming-pellet containment buildings were unmistakable, garishly colored, and sported tall chimneys that belched incandescent flames at all hours of the day and night. Peregrine parked the flaming-pellet wagon at the nearest loading dock, leaving them with their final task of the day, removing the empty hotboxes and depositing them in the containment building's exchange room.

"Heard you ran into some excitement," Mangrove said, walking up to them while they were still loading the hotboxes onto a flatbed dolly. Peregrine and Mangrove had history, people lumping them together because they had similar family names—Volker and Hatfield-Volker—even though they were not related. Nobody cared, lumping them anyway. There were many extended families that made up Clan Melaleuca, living and working on the sprawling farming complex. Lumping them was easy, which drove Peregrine and Mangrove to distraction.

"Heard that, did you?" Peregrine said. Heath kept his thoughts to himself.

"Something about a rogue goat." Mangrove watched them, hand on hip. As was tradition, she made absolutely no move to help them with the hotboxes or the cart.

"There may have been a goat."

"I knew it," Mangrove turned. "Hey Queue."

"Christ," Heath muttered to nobody in particular. Peregrine heard but didn't comment.

Queue Hatfield-Volker sauntered over. Queue and Mangrove were sisters, working the flaming-pellet wagons. They were a good team.

"It's true," Mangrove said.

"Told you it was true," Queue replied, sounding smug.

"Word travels faster than we can shovel it." Peregrine closed the side of the flaming-pellet wagon. Door rattled shut with a satisfying *thunk*.

"Heard it was a kid." Queue continued to sound smugly satisfied with herself, sauntering along while Peregrine and Heath maneuvered the cart.

"That was the weirdest part," Peregrine said over her shoulder, pushing. Heath tried to ignore them.

"It's certainly unusual." Mangrove strolled along as well, keeping up with her sister.

"Would have caught me by surprise," Queue said.

"Not the goat."

"No, definitely not the goat," Queue replied. "All the fire and wanton destruction, kind of a giveaway there's a goat in the neighborhood."

"Actually, that may have been the weirdest part," Peregrine said as if she might turn.

"What part?"

"The lack of devastation." Peregrine stopped, put a hand to her forehead, looked to Heath. He shrugged a sigh, pressing onward without her aid, but otherwise kept his thoughts to himself. "Wasn't that weird?" she said, trying to capture his attention.

Heath stopped—the cart would have to fend for itself—and stood slowly as if his back hurt and he was getting ready to stretch. He felt his muscles ache and his chest burn.

"There was the fire," he finally said.

"Yeah, but that was blocks away," Peregrine countered. She spread her fingers, moving hands apart as if indicating distance. "Goats tend to leave an uninterrupted trail."

"There's a perfectly reasonable explanation," Ash November said. They all turned at his voice, spinning, startled, nobody having noticed his approach. "The goat trials are immanent," he continued, walking toward them. They wanted to scatter. Ash was Marshall November's nephew. He was learning the reed pipes and was well on his way to becoming a reed master. Great things were planned for him. "Another clan was trying to snipe our business, showing a baby goat around."

"Not a bright idea," Heath said. Nobody else wanted to speak.

"No," Ash said, scanning their faces as if looking for doubt, and then settled on Heath. "A moment of your time," he said.

"That sounds officious," Heath replied, Peregrine moving to his side.

"Finish with the cart," Ash said in her general direction.

"It's a two-man job," she countered.

"They can help you," indicating Mangrove and Queue.

"She said *two man*," Queue replied.

"Yeah." Mangrove didn't want her opinion left out of the discussion.

"I'm sure the three of you can make up the difference." Ash turned, squashing the last of their defiance. "This way," said to Heath without looking back.

Heath and Peregrine shared a look. Heath attempted a helpless shrug of shoulders, arms haphazardly raised and quickly dropped. Peregrine bit off a sigh before it could take flight and motioned for him to follow after the future reed master and clan leader.

"Where are you taking me?" Heath asked only after they had been walking for a slight slip of time, trundling down some seldom-used passage or other that he didn't recognize.

Ash turned, looking, and tried to give Heath half a smile. Failing that, Ash took Heath in his arms—there was nobody about—and kissed him.

"Wanted a moment to myself," he said. They were an unpublicized item, reed master and dung shoveler existing in different clan social strata. Empty hallways came in handy.

"That doesn't fill me with confidence." Heath let his

arms linger around Ash's back, fingers stroking, and tried without much success to hold Ash's gaze.

"Your stunt with the reed pipes was noticed."

"That," looking away, "isn't much of a surprise."

"What were you thinking?"

"That I wanted to help," pulling away. Ash caught his arms, hands drifting, fingers lingering together, Heath letting the moment breathe.

"Wanting isn't enough," Ash finally said. "Look what happened."

"I know."

"I know you know," leaning in, kissing him again. "We'll get through this."

"We will?"

"Yes," attempting another smile. "We will."

They walked, arms linked, hand in hand, but drifting apart as soon as they found themselves in less-deserted confines. The halls were paneled wood, cheerfully painted, and the floors were scattered with straw. Nobody knew why. Lights had been stuck on the walls as if an afterthought. The building was old enough that electricity had been considered a luxury of the times.

Ash stopped before one door, people moving around them. He took a moment, looking Heath over as if he might have said something, had there been fewer people about. Heath wondered if his heart was beating. He couldn't feel it. He could not find his breath. Ash closed his eyes for just a moment and then pushed open the door.

The office looked as if a paper and confetti bomb had once been set off within its confines and nobody had noticed. There were books, documents, and crumpled paper everywhere. Even the floor was covered, boot prints having placed their collective stamp upon mislaid forms and documents. There was a table that sort of resembled a desk, having been intended as a temporary measure made permanent from the weight of files. Half-open windows overlooked the goat paddocks. The sounds and sulfurous smells of the fire-breathing goats were unmistakable.

Marshall November was there, which wasn't much of a surprise. Heath's uncle, Vladimir Cyclone, was also there, which was more unsettling than surprising. Vladimir seldom had a word for him, much less a kind one, and the day's excitement did not lead Heath to think kind words were imminent. Aides, assistants, and functionaries were there, circling around the clan leaders, devouring their attention. Marshall eventually noticed that Heath and his nephew had appeared.

"Give us a moment," Marshall said. The functionaries and assistants departed with quiet efficiency, leaving Heath alone with Ash and the clan leaders.

Heath knew he should say something but felt lost to the world and drowning in a sea of empty air. They seemed inclined to let him flounder, which made the burnt char that was all that remained of his heart feel worse. His uncle hadn't bothered to look up from the assorted notices and reports spread before him.

"Any leads?" Ash started to ask, trailing away quickly under Marshall's gaze.

Heath wanted to speak, finding nothing. They weren't even looking at him.

"There was little of anything left," Marshall said. "The goat saw to that."

"And the goat too young for brands or marks," Vladimir added without disturbing his study of the day's reports.

"None of which was Heathcliff's fault," Ash said.

"Two months." Vladimir's voice was a knife.

"I'm . . . sorry?" Ash said, sounding genuinely puzzled. "I don't—"

"Unlicensed reed pipes."

"They're not unlicensed," Heath said, wanting to scream, his voice a whispered whip, his words an intrusion as if everyone had forgotten that he could speak. Silence followed, lingered.

"They're not licensed to you," Marshall finally said, looking directly at him. "Two months confinement for unlawful use—"

"Unlawful?"

"Yes." His voice was hard. "The damage that can be done. You saw it," pointing. "The danger to people's lives."

Heath was quiet, studying the tabletop, seeing nothing.

"The reason there's nobody to question about the goat," Vladimir said.

"That's not—" Heath started, stopped, looked up. "I didn't cause that."

"No," Marshall said. "You just made it worse."

"Two months," Heath whispered without air, seeking a chair, knowing he wouldn't reach one if he tried. "I'll miss the goat trials."

"There must be something," Ash said, speaking as if he might reach for Heath, hold him.

"There is," Marshall said. Heath closed his eyes.

"Surrender the unlicensed reeds," Vladimir said. He had yet to dignify Heath with a look or even a glance.

"They're not unlicensed," Heath said, feeling the world tremble and sway.

"To your mother," Vladimir said. "My sister."

"My father." Heath held the table, and Vladimir did finally look at him.

"Arturo Claymore never owned reed pipes once in his life."

"I said *my father*."

They studied each other across the table, Heath clinging to its edge.

"Nobody knows your father," Marshall said but quietly.

"Which is why you cannot take them," Heath replied.

"Rainchild Cyclone-Claymore is a reed master," Marshall said. "She's always owned reeds."

"Please," a word.

"Two months, then," Vladimir said.

"Lady Rainchild," Ash said as if shouting for everyone to stop without actually shouting. They looked to him. "What if we returned the reeds to Lady Rainchild?"

"They do belong to her." Marshall sounded reasonable.

Heath felt everyone watching him, their gazes turning, as if the weight of their combined attention would bore him into the ground, smothering.

"It's not what I would want," all but gasping, struggling for air.

"Then it's settled," Vladimir said. "We will return the reeds to their rightful owner."

"No," barely a whisper.

Marshall drew a slow breath as if stalling for time, the sound of it holding Vladimir back. Nobody spoke.

"This is where we started," Vladimir finally said.

"It's the handing over," Heath managed to say, rumbling quietly. "Never see them again."

"An issue of trust?" Marshall sounded as if he stood at the very edge of patience.

"No."

"I can take them," Ash said, speaking over Heath's lonesome word before it could find purchase in the hard edges of the others' minds. "Lady Rainchild knows me. I think I can be trusted."

"It's not what I would want," Vladimir said, voice at the edge of growling.

"Then it's settled," Marshall said. "Ash will escort Heathcliff to his mother. The reed pipes handed over. Confinement avoided. The trials attended."

"The trials attended," Heath whispered. Ash clasped him on the shoulder, hand clamping down. Heath very nearly jumped at the touch.

"Come," Ash said, meaning they should hurry before one or the other of their uncles should change their mind, and they did leave, Heath moving slowly, following. "That could have gone much worse," Ash said when they were far from the offices, functionaries, and potential for prying ears.

Heath did not answer.

Ash let the silence drift while continuing to lead Heath through the labyrinth that was the clan's farming complex. Heath's mother did not participate in the more communal aspects of the clan's facilities. It required a car and a bit of a drive to reach her.

Ash drove, keeping half an eye on Heath.

"It won't be that bad," Ash finally said, words falling into the distant silence. "I'm sure the sixty days . . . And they will let you reclaim your father's reeds."

"The goat trials," Heath said. "The reed pipe chorus. I was going to participate. First time, remember?"

"I remember." He had forgotten.

"You promised."

"Did more than promise." Eyes only for the road, promise having slipped his mind.

"Without reed pipes—" Let his hands flutter and flail. "They don't hand those out, you know."

"I know."

"Like they planned it," looking out the window. "Out of the goat trials—"

"You're attending the trials," interrupting.

"Out of the chorus," defiant.

Ash started to counter, speaking before the words

could form, and then seemed to catch himself as if noticing the lack of preparation in his thoughts.

"I doubt they planned it," he finally said, risking a glance at Heath.

"Target of opportunity," Heath muttered, gathering silence as if he would wrap himself in it like a shroud. "*Nobody knows your father,*" mocking. "Like I could forget," said while stretching out his arms, looking to the symbols and patterns running their length. The tattoos had been an involuntary addition ordered by his uncle and resembled nothing so much as lightning dancing with fire. "Like I've been painted in mud."

"The finest ink, surely," Ash countered.

"That's an improvement?"

"Been drinking mud?"

"Not lately."

"It's an improvement."

"Take your word for it," said while folding his arms over his chest, squeezing as if desperate to keep warm. "When were you drinking mud?"

"Well, it wasn't so much *drinking,*" Ash said, drawing the words out, glancing at Heath, who was continuing to cocoon himself in his own thoughts. "Look, you have fallen into mud before, yes?"

"Face first?"

"Of course face first, how else would it get in my mouth?"

"Someone could have thrown it at you," Heath said, sounding reasonable.

"Someone suicidal," sounding indignant. "So given what we do, working with pyromaniacal goats, diving face first into mud shouldn't sound that unusual."

"Best antidote for a fiery death," Heath muttered, his gaze drifting back to the window. His hand reached for the pouch at his side, touching the reed pipes, remembering fire blossoming all around him.

Rainchild Cyclone-Claymore lived in a nice part of town. The streets were paved. The sidewalks were wide. Hedges fenced the large houses and homes as if trying to hide the fire walls—red brick and stone—protection from errant flame that could strike without warning.

"I feel like I was just here," Heath said as they passed the gates of his mother's home. There was considerable resemblance to the mansions of the day's deliveries.

The place was a sprawling multilayered affair that had been half-converted into a school. His mother had once explained that she simply did not need the space anymore, and it got the children away from the Clan Melaleuca complex. It also exposed them to children from other parts of the city.

They left the car with a chauffeur and were admitted to the residence proper by a housemaid who was all shy smiles and quiet courtesy. They were offered coffee and left to wait in a pleasant parlor with comfortable chairs. The inescapable sounds of children could be heard like the patter of summer rain off in the distance.

"I'm sorry to keep you waiting," Rainchild said, sweeping into the parlor. She was a rush of wind lifting them to their feet despite their desire for the chairs, which really were quite comfortable. "I wasn't expecting," crossing to Heath, taking his hands. "It's not your day for lessons."

Heath tried to speak, failed.

"It's nice to see you, Lady Rainchild," Ash said but quietly.

"And you, Young Master Ash," sounding puzzled, looking between them. "Do you need the suite? I could arrange to be elsewhere. The children always need something."

"No," Heath said, scandalized, all but speaking over her, "but thank you."

"Then what has happened?" looking between them, gripping his hands. "Something has happened?"

"I'm surprised you don't know," muttered. "Word travels faster than we can shovel it."

"There's a reason I am so far from the center of commerce and industry." She let their fingers drift apart, walked to one of the chairs, and took her time arranging herself into it as if she was wearing an elaborate gown that could not abide wrinkles. "The rumors, scuttlebutt, and lies, that was my husband's game."

"It was at that," Ash said, "and he loved it, I remember."

"And he loved me enough to grant me all of this," moving her hand slowly about as if giving a tour, taking in items of particular interest. Arturo Claymore had been a braggart and fast talker, spreading stories of Clan Melaleuca far and wide, but he had never been accepted as a clan leader.

"There is a reason we are here," Ash said, "unfortunately."

Heath took the pouch slung over his shoulder and moved, all but staggering as if he would fall. They watched him, silent.

"I fear I have been unwise." Heath placed the reed pipes in the chair next to her.

"But the goat trials," she said. "The reed pipe chorus."

"Your brother's idea," Ash said as if embarrassed.

"My brother," said as if choking back bile that would burn the rug and eat through the floor. She had not spoken to him since the day he had ordered the tattoos etched and scarred into Heath's arms.

"Surrender the reeds or face two months' confinement."

"I see," burning.

"I only wanted to help," Heath managed.

"There was a rogue goat," Ash said, explaining, "on Heath's rounds delivering the flaming pellets."

"Are you hurt?" Rainchild said, grabbing Heath's arm, turning it this way and that as if searching the marks for fresh burns.

"I'm fine," pulling away, stalking the room. "It got away from me."

"You're not ready," she said as if she would reach for him.

"Obviously," said with a spark of fire.

"Who's your delivery partner? Peregrine? She has no talent."

"She knew better than to try." He continued to stalk the room as if he would smash the first thing heavy enough to cause actual structural damage to the building.

"Punishment," Ash said, watching him, but speaking to Rainchild. "Vladimir has wanted an excuse to take those reeds for a long time. This was it," pointing to where they lay neglected in the depths of a chair. "Handing them over to you was the only compromise I could manage."

"Thank you," Rainchild said, her hand drifting, touching the reeds. "These belonged to your father."

"I know," Heath replied as if breathing hurt, turning on her. "That's all anybody knows."

"I am sorry," said to Heath. "And you are right," said to Ash. "This is punishment . . . my punishment . . . because I cannot say more about the father of my indiscretion."

"Cannot," Heath said, and there really wasn't anything more to say.

Meetings

The goat trials arrived, time slipping past in an instant. Heath and Peregrine had followed their rounds, the days dragging one into another, Peregrine driving, speaking to the groundskeepers and household staff, Heath helping with the hotboxes, watching the world through the half-open window of the shotgun seat.

The goat trials were held in the high coliseum on the waterfront, far from Clan Melaleuca's stronghold. The high coliseum's floors were hard clay. The walls were cold stone. When the people cheered, the stadium roared like a great untidy gong that could be heard for miles around.

The high coliseum complex was a collection of six arenas, varying sizes. The smaller courts held the younger and less-skilled trials, minimizing the risk to random spectators should any actually be in attendance. The larger arenas showcased the older and more experienced trials, where there may have been less risk to the audience but the fiery explosions were far more spectacular. Peregrine and Heath had found seats overlooking the largest arena.

"Who's next?" Peregrine asked as the field was cleared.

"I think it's another from Clan Welwitschia," Heath answered.

"They suck," she said, turning toward the field, voice rising. "They should be fed to their goats and then boiled in their own rendered oil, in that order."

"That is not in the spirit of the peace."

"It's all in the spirit of the peace." She had been drinking. "We are all one big happy family."

"Family is no guarantee of peace." They had all been drinking.

The goatherd clans were fiercely competitive, especially where customers and territory were concerned. Encounters between clans typically ended violently. The goat trials were one of the few places where clan members coming face to face did not end with bloody knuckles and broken bones.

"Bring forth the Clan Melaleuca quality," Peregrine roared.

A goatherd entered the ring to a swirling bedlam of jeering and cheering voices. He wore a slick coat and hood. It was hard to tell one contestant from another. He held reed pipes carved of white bone. A gate was raised. A blast of air pushed a goat into the ring. The fire-breathing goat of death quietly surveyed the field with hatred in its heart and vexation in its eyes at the cacophony of sound raining down around it. The air began to blister and burn.

The goatherd had only to quiet the goat with the reed pipes. It was only the first day of the first round of the trials. The goatherd faced only one goat. Thick shields of well-tempered and fire-resistant glass helped protect the spectators from the possibility of fiery death should the goatherd not do well.

The Clan Welwitschia goatherd did well. Cheering outpaced the uncritically disdainful factions of the crowd as the goatherd left the field.

"Where's Ash November?" Peregrine shouted. "When's Ash November?"

"He'll be here soon enough," Heath said.

Other clan members took up the chant for the reed master and future clan leader to hasten his arrival to the arena floor. Heath left after Ash's very good show-ing.

There were hallways, antechambers, and dressing rooms swirling around and beneath the arena where the contestants gathered, preparing for their turn in the trials, reveling in their successes, recovering from their failures. Trainers, teachers, and mentors were there, breathing rarefied air. Family and loved ones might be waiting, should duties or responsibility allow.

Heath knew the way. Once upon a time, he had au-ditioned for the reed pipe chorus and even attended rehearsals in chambers that surrounded the coliseum. Now, he stood in cold hallways, feeling stone walls be-neath his fingers. He could hear cheering. He could feel laughter.

Heath had only to follow one hallway, one flight of stairs, another narrower stairway, and then say that he was from Clan Melaleuca with a message for the future clan leader. He could say he was waiting for his turn in the trials, seeking guidance or last-minute advice from this master or that trainer. He could say almost anything, gain admittance, but he only wandered the hallways, turning, climbing stairs, seeking rafters.

The high coliseum was like a great cauldron during the day, while the trials lasted, everyone swirling, chanting and cheering, wanting to be as close to the arena floor as possible. The people pushed forward. They pressed down, watching the trials, staying close to the action. Nobody pulled away, wanting the empty clouds and the silent sky. None sought the quiet soli-tude floating above it all.

The rafters were lost and empty while the day last-ed. That would change. After the sun set and the light faded, the rafters would fill with people seeking each other in the quiet and the dark. It was part of the peace that extended over the trials and the gathering of clans.

People who would never otherwise meet found each other in the twilight world floating over all.

The rafters were a catacomb of small rooms and chambers, strewn with soft bedding and straw, welcoming and comforting. The rafters were only quiet while the sun shone and the people cheered below.

Heath found space among the rafters, folded himself into a corner, rested his head against the wall. It was quiet. The chambers really were set up for comfort. The crowds, cheering, were a soft rumble like the distant call of a forgotten storm, and then there were other sounds, rustling, almost voices, moaning.

Heath felt a smile, accepting that even the rafters were never truly empty. He stood, moving slowly, seeking more distant spaces.

"What's that?" a voice, uncertain, speaking softly.

"Someone there?" another.

"Join us," maybe the first voice or possibly even a third.

Soft laughter followed, and Heath let it drift behind him, seeking other chambers. He sought rooms in the very heights of the catacombs, away from the quietly inviting voices, and as far away from the cheering crowds as he thought it possible to go. Since his first guess for solitude had proven slightly less than true, he could only hope that his second would prove more secluded given the hour. Soon enough, the day's trials would end, and the evening's feasting would begin.

There were banquet halls with long tables among the many spaces of the high coliseum. There were benches. Chandeliers suspended from the ceiling held lights crafted to resemble candles and lost stars. Food would be provided—exquisite meals, held in common for all who attended the trials.

There would be music. The reed chorus would migrate from banquet room to feasting hall, playing as they went. They would perform, pausing here, moving there, and the revelers would applaud, listening with half an ear between bites of food and sips of beer.

Only after, there would be dancing, and then the mingled members of the various clans would begin to take an interest in the opportunities the rafters provided. People enjoying the freedom—or at least relative anonymity—of the softly prepared and twilight-dark rooms that were the rafters.

Heath had time. He could still see the sun drifting low through the sky, and he could still feel, more than hear, the low rumbling of the crowds around the arenas and trials. He closed his eyes, feeling the cold, desiring silence, but found none. Then, growing softly, slipping past the distant roar and rumble of the people far below, he heard the lonesome sound of a reed pipe like a whispered breath echoing through the empty air.

He felt more than heard the haunting melody, sounding like a lost secret wanting to remain hidden from the world but crying to the hollow spaces all the same. The reed song called to him like an ache he could not describe, feeling it in his heart and deep in his bones.

The song pulled at him, and he found himself seeking it without even realizing that he was moving, wandering from lost chamber to forgotten room in the farthest heights of the catacombs. The melancholy tune slipped away like a sigh run out of time at last, and Heath thought he would die, feeling the ache in his soul, trembling.

The memory of the tune as it had echoed around him refused to leave him, and he pressed deeper into the catacombs, searching, seeking, finding nothing. Turning this way and that in the half shadow and quiet tombs, he feared he was lost.

Heath held his breath, feeling the world ache like a

swelling in his chest, and just as he thought he could stand it no longer, a new song touched him. Again, it was a whisper wishing not to be heard but dreaming for attention all the same. It was so close, Heath moved, very nearly running, stumbling.

He found the reed master, sitting alone in spaces that Heath had not even known existed in the heights and spires of the high coliseum. The man stopped, reeds dropping to his lap the second Heath stumbled upon his hiding place. The reed master said nothing. He did not even move, watching Heath at the edge of the chamber as if he might bolt at the slightest provocation.

"Please," Heath managed to say. His voice was a husk of raw straw and burnt dust. He wanted to say so much more, but his voice slipped away entirely, leaving him nothing.

The reed master watched him, swallowing his heart, looking as if he could not breathe, and then his eyes darted like frightened children to the reed pipes in his lap. Heath said nothing. The reed master lifted the reeds, slowly, awkwardly, as if they might burn, and then he brought them to his lips. He began to play.

Trembling, Heath thought he would fall, the floor taking him, but he managed to step toward the music. It was soft like a breath of wind not wanting to be heard. It was a soulful ache of misplaced folly. It was beautiful.

Heath did collapse, all but falling at the reed master's feet, drawing the man's attention. The music stopped, echoes drifting around them, slipping away, never heard again.

"What was that?" Heath's voice scratched at his throat, and he realized that he had been crying.

"I do not know," the reed master said, and his voice

was a dry ache so much like Heath's own. "But it was mine."

"I am yours," Heath said, trying to breathe. "I am Heathcliff—"

"No, no," interrupting, scolding with a finger. "That is not in the spirit of the revelries."

"They are still at the games."

The man seemed to consider Heath's words. "True," he finally said and then seemed to consider some more. "Chardonnay," motioning to himself with the reed pipes.

"Chardonnay," Heath repeated the name, accepting it.

"I thought I had privacy," taking in the space, meaning the catacombs entire.

"I thought I had solitude," leaning back, watching Chardonnay.

"We are clearly foolish children."

"Clearly."

"I sought solitude," Chardonnay said, lifting the reed pipes as if presenting them to Heath. "My voice is unwelcome."

"Your voice is beautiful."

"Did you recognize the tune?" Chardonnay asked. "Of course not. It did not follow any of the accepted strictures. It is worthless for charming the wild goats."

"I am worthless," Heath said, choking, words catching in his throat. "I cannot calm even an unruly kid."

"Nobody's worthless." Chardonnay raised the reed pipes, began to play softly.

The sound was joyous, barely heard, like the laughter of children playing in a distant garden. It pulled at Heath's heart. The breath pushed at the boundaries of his chest as if seeking to escape directly through the gaps in his ribs rather than flow from between his lips.

Chardonnay stopped, abruptly, and Heath thought he would suffocate, never able to draw breath again.

"Was that worthless?" Chardonnay asked. "The goats care nothing for it. Perchance that is why you could not calm even an unruly kid, playing songs they cannot hear."

"You played that for them?" Heath said, taking in the pipes, meaning the song.

Chardonnay chuckled without sound, shoulders hiccupping, as if voicing a quiet *harrumph*. "Maybe," he said.

"Your teachers must not have liked that."

"They did not," Chardonnay said with quiet resignation.

"And yet they let you keep your reeds."

"Well," drawing the word out, "it was not recently, and they may not have actually been there when I made the attempt."

"That must have been . . ." Heath said, blinking, picturing Chardonnay sneaking into goat pens in the middle of the night. "That must have been something."

"I've learned my lesson," Chardonnay said, looking about, Heath following his gaze, taking in the hidden chambers of the high catacombs with his eyes.

"They must cheer for you in the trials."

"They do."

"A great audience."

"I prefer this one." Chardonnay stretched out a hand as if he would pull Heath to his feet.

Heath did move, accepting space on the bench at Chardonnay's side. Their shoulders brushed together. The bench wasn't that wide.

"The reeds make my mouth warm," Chardonnay said. They kissed.

"I may have something to quench that." Heath

moved their hands to his lap, fingers linking, entwining, quietly moving.

"You may," Chardonnay replied.

Even with the extra fingers in the way, teasing, Heath found the buckles and clasps at his waist easy to unbind. His trousers slipped away, sliding down his hips. Heath shifted on the bench, Chardonnay's fingers lingering, stroking. The reed master moved, kneeling before him, hands touching, revealing, lips brushing Heath's thighs.

A soft moan escaped Heath, inviting, feeling Chardonnay explore, finding so much more. Heath felt his legs yielding, drifting away, granting Chardonnay space to roam.

Chardonnay let his hand drift to his own trousers, fumbling at the bindings and clasps. While Chardonnay's mouth was occupied and Heath could reach only so far as to tousle and stroke the reed master's hair, Chardonnay worked his trousers free and began to stroke.

Chardonnay stopped his tongue's and lips' exploration and gentle performance. He moaned, almost a gasp, and then he looked up, meeting Heath's eyes.

"You were very warm," Heath said, teasing.

"Playing has that effect upon me," was the reply.

"You are a talented performer," smiling.

"There's an encore," Chardonnay said, raising his hand, brushing it slowly over Heath's skin, seeking, finding.

Chardonnay let his fingers encircle, softly, gently gripping, and then his lips lightly touching, kissing the tip. The hand began to move in quick, short strokes, while his mouth enveloped. Heath closed his eyes, hands falling away, fingers trembling, unable to hold or caress Chardonnay's face with his fingertips.

Warmth flowed through Heath like a breath drawn deep and held until he thought he might die.

Chardonnay rested back on his knees, looking up at Heath, fingers lingering, drifting slowly. Heath felt his heart swirl and start to beat like slow drops of water striking a pond.

"A fine encore," Heath said.

"An appreciative audience is its own reward."

They let the moment drift, listening to the distant cheers, feeling the rumble and call of the voices far below. There were adjustments to clothing to be made, attempts to appear more presentable, clean up a bit.

"A connoisseur of the reeds," Chardonnay said. "I should have recognized the signs."

"Following such music, seeking the reed master, wasn't enough of a clue?"

"I don't know about *master*," sounding wistful.

"I assure you it is true of more than one thing."

"As a follower of the dancing men, you would know better than I."

"No," Heath said, a short sharp sound. "I am no friend of the dancing men."

"Oh, I thought," Chardonnay said, stumbling. "The ink."

Heath drew his arms closed, pulling at his sleeves as if he might somehow better cover the tattoos.

"I should go," he said.

"Oh, they were not." Chardonnay let his voice drift away before the thought could flounder and flail upon the cold floor.

Heath did not answer, finding his voice turned to stone in his throat, threatening to burst, blood flowing from the gaping wound below his jaw. He fled the hardening comforts at the very pinnacle of the catacombs—no one following him—thinking never to return.

Flirtations

Breakfast was a communal affair that took place at cafeterias scatted throughout the Clan Melaleuca farming complex. Living accommodations resembled apartments with shared common areas. Four single or double bedrooms split a living room, kitchenette, and bathroom. Snacks and evening meals were prepared locally and enjoyed in the shared living space. Arguments over what to have on the telly involved only a small group, but breakfast was altogether different.

Breakfast was buffet-style cafeteria fare. People pointed. Food was slopped into a flat bowl by jaded and disillusioned staff. End results were handed over the counter.

There was scrambled egg. There was sausage. There was toast. There was sausage and egg on toast. Fruit juice was from concentrate resembling a dense semi-sweet sludge. Coffee was black. Everyone agreed that the coffee was black.

Breakfast trays were then taken to four-to-six-person tables that had been rammed end to end so long ago that few remembered they could be broken into smaller units. Nobody bothered their table mates, so it didn't really matter.

"You vanished early," Peregrine said, dropping into the chair next to Heath, letting her tray clatter to the tabletop. She took the opportunity to lean heavily against him, shoulder brushing shoulder as she slouched into her seat.

"Not that early," Heath replied. The revelries ran to all hours of the night, but people were still expected to sleep it off at home. Peregrine and Heath shared a common room. He hadn't noticed her return.

"Well, you certainly made your own way last night."

"It worked out," which was true. Heath had enjoyed the revelries. It had just taken him a little longer than normal to get into the spirit of the evening after leaving Chardonnay of the unknown last name.

"That's good," Peregrine said. The food smeared before them on the trays existed mostly to be glared at and occasionally prodded with a spoon. Conversation could distract and delay the inevitable. "My night was not without excitement."

"As was to be expected." Heath tried a sip of coffee, mostly as a way to avoid sampling the sausage-and-egg concoction on his plate that was slowly mutating into a wholly new life form hellbent on seeking vengeance against its oppressors. Coffee was definitely black.

"Not without much excitement at all." She seemed to be after more than an excuse to avoid breakfast. Subtle inquiries into how his evening had gone were not her strong suit.

"If you are fishing for hangover cures, I'm fresh out."

"I'm not fishing," said with an edgy sigh that drifted into silence. "Secret is to stay hydrated," she mumbled.

"I didn't cry in a corner, if that was the concern," Heath said. It was her concern. She was crap at asking. He hadn't wanted to divulge. "It worked out. Even met somebody." This last revelation trailing away into mumbling of his own.

"Yeah?" Peregrine brightened like a fire-breathing goat of death kindling flame. "Did you get a name? At revelries?"

"Not that uncommon to get a name." It was very uncommon.

"Details," said while grabbing his arm. "Don't make me start with my own."

"Not in the spirit of the revelries," he countered, which was kind of true. Details risked spoiling anonymity. "Besides, it might upset their breakfast," meaning their neighbors of the table.

"It's all in the spirit of the revelries," mumbling, accepting they were not alone.

Faces turned back to various and sundry trays resting before them. Heath had to admit that it had been impossible to avoid the reed chorus as they had traveled from feasting hall to revelry room, which had added a note of wistful melancholy to his evening. The music had echoed. The memory of it reverberated behind his eyes and between his ears. There had been other music—he would never forget—in the high catacombs, haunting, lonely.

"Do you—" he started to say, startling Peregrine almost as much as himself. "Do you ever think about the music?"

"No."

"Did it seem . . . I don't know . . . did it seem . . . off?"

"Why in tarnation would it seem off?" She had to put her spoon down.

"I don't know," said feeling sheepish with Peregrine staring at him. "Must have been drinking."

"Goes without saying."

Breakfast also went without saying. Taste and desire notwithstanding, they finished their food in as timely a fashion as they could manage, wanting to get back to the high coliseum complex for day two of the goat trials. There were clan members to cheer and other clans to boo. Objects would need to be thrown. Streamers and toilet paper were popular options in order to keep clan rivalries within the spirit of the peace.

Ash November made another very good showing. He was well on his way to being a tournament champion. Watching reed masters made Heath think once more of his companion of the rafters.

Heath abandoned his compatriots, using some excuse or other having to do with the pressure of too much alcohol on the bladder. They had all been drinking—it started early—so the excuse was readily accepted.

He wanted—he didn't know what he wanted—to learn the clan affiliation of his mystery reed master, and he sought the detailed rolls and schedules that were available in the tournament spaces below the arena floor. The programs handed out in the auditorium were little more than scraps of paper with only the most basic information.

Heath knew the way, descending stairs he had avoided only the day before, and sought the scheduling office. It would be busy, hectic people flying, raised voices screaming. Heath had high if potentially misguided hopes of going unnoticed amidst the scrum.

He ran into Ash November's entourage, family, fellow reed students, and assorted hangers-on. He all but ran into Ash. The collision was not without mishap, but they recovered quickly. The problem was that reed masters and goat-dung shovelers were not supposed to mix.

"Watch where you are going," someone said, sounding like Cassandra Laughingstock. Heath kept his head down.

"It's quite all right," Ash said. "We have followers of all sorts."

"They should follow from a distance," definitely Cassandra.

"It may be a message from my uncle." Ash took Heath's arm with the practiced ease of someone knowing they should not show familiarity. "Privacy may be required," looking to the others over Heath's bowed head. "You will have to excuse me."

The entourage and assorted tournament participants nodded and grumbled their understanding. Ash and Heath were able to move away from the throng, finding quiet hallways deep below the arena floor.

"Of all the audacity," Ash said. "I should be quite cross with you."

"It was not my intention," Heath tried to say, stumbling over words like wooden blocks scattered across the floor, realizing that Ash still wore his goat-trial gear. He smelled like fresh earth and cold fire.

"I like the audacity," touching Heath's face with gloved fingertips. "Spirit of the revelries."

"Spirit of the revelries would be finding you in the rafters," trying to smile.

"That would be," leaning into him, "very nearly acceptable."

There was quiet kissing, lips brushing together. There was delicate hunger. Drinking him in, Ash smelled like old smoke scented with rosewater.

"The gloves," Ash said, reaching down, fumbling with clasps. "I don't know." His knee was between Heath's legs, pushing slowly. Heath tried to grip Ash's leg with his thighs. "Are they soft?"

Ash's fingers slipped into Heath's pants, seeking, searching, finding. Heath tried not to gasp, failing, breath escaping in a rush.

"Yes," Heath managed. The gloves were supple but hard, soft enough to hold and work the reed pipes but strong enough to protect against pyrokinetic-goat flame.

He reached, stretching, hands sliding down Ash's

arms and across his waist. There was fumbling with clasps. His trousers refused to fall, Ash's leg holding them suspended. He managed Ash's fastenings open. Ash pressed against him, brushing against his thigh.

They locked eyes, breathing hard, tasting each other's breath. Heath's hands slid around Ash's waist, finding his back. He wondered if they had the corridor to themselves.

He tried not to cry out, fingers slipping, lowering his head as if he could not hold it upright, forehead pressing against Ash's own. Brushing cheeks together, Ash held himself against Heath, moving softly but urgently.

Ash gasped, fighting his own breath, kissing Heath's shoulder as if desperate to bite him so that he would not cry out. They stood locked together, no longer moving, trembling. Heath wanted to slip to the floor. Locked together, they held each other against the wall.

At last, they did settle to the cold stone, sitting together, leaning their backs against the wall, and Heath started to laugh, a slow chuckle that threatened to grow.

"What?" Ash asked, his voice a teasing whisper. Heath shook his head, catching at his breath.

"This was," Heath tried to say, staggering under his own thoughts, "not planned."

"You weren't looking for me?"

"I don't know what," tripping over his own words, stopping. "Do you ever think about the music?"

"I don't," Ash began, puzzled. "That's an odd question."

Heath raised his hands, helpless, fighting with his thoughts, and let them flop back to his lap. "What's it all about?" he managed.

"And that's a non sequitur," turning, trying to study Heath more carefully.

"The music," hearing melodies echo in the dark recesses of his mind. "What's it for?"

"To charm and control the goats. That's not exactly a mystery."

"Is that all?" feeling desperate, feeling cold, even as the words escaped him.

"It's not exactly easy," Ash said. "You know that."

"I know that."

"Isn't it enough?" he asked, brushing Heath's face, running fingers through his hair. The touch was soft, gentle, warm. Heath wanted to press his face into Ash's palm.

"I don't know." Heath's voice was barely a whisper.

"This is about—dammit." The last was an exhalation of breath, stumbling over how to frame words. "This is about the goat you couldn't control—"

"No—"

"I think it is," Ash said, holding his voice soft, firm. He took Heath's arm, pulled back the sleeve, touched the jagged spirals and frayed markings. "I really think it is."

"Isn't—" Heath felt that if he started to cry, he would never stop. "They took my father's reeds."

"I know—damnation," looking away. "I have—" took a deep breath. "I've been away from the others too long." Ash meant his fellow participants in the tournament. Heath knew it. Ash had responsibilities as a future reed master and clan leader. "I have to—"

"I know," Heath said through closed eyes.

"Lady Rainchild should be here," Ash said. "She's performing tonight."

"I actually knew that."

"You should go," voice trailing away. "Do you know the way?"

"I know the way."

Rainchild Cyclone-Claymore was an honored guest

of the goat trials because of her mastery of the reed pipes and her dedication to teaching the reeds regardless of clan affiliation. There were expansive suites and rooms set aside for such guests that were only loosely connected to the high coliseum complex. Heath knew the way and found himself without too much difficulty being presented to his mother in a gloriously opulent sitting room.

There were reclining chairs with crushed silk and velvet cushions. There was a coffee service spread upon an intricately carved table. There was a three-tier tray fashionably arrayed with sandwiches, sweets, and pastries.

His mother looked like a visiting dignitary, holding court from the comfort of one of the chairs with a cup and saucer situated within easy reach. She also looked as if she had been valiantly working to maintain perfect posture for quite some time and was growing tired of it.

Chardonnay was there, which threw Heath so badly that he very nearly stumbled into the room. His mother and Chardonnay faced each other from opposing chairs, with the coffee service between them as if it was a makeshift chessboard.

"You have company, of course," Heath managed to say. "I should not intrude."

"Nonsense," Rainchild said, rising, crossing to him. Chardonnay rose to his feet as if an echo of her movements. "You are most welcome." Hands on his shoulders, she graced him with air kisses, one for each cheek. "The company is Chardonnay Chalice, Clan Amaryllis. I do not think you have met."

"I would have remembered," Heath said, trying to hide that he now had a name and clan affiliation to go with his reed master of the day before.

"One of my best students," she said, facing Chardonnay. "Formerly."

"Once upon a time," Chardonnay said but quietly. He also appeared to be doing mental gymnastics.

"He developed ideas," she said over her shoulder to Heath as if Chardonnay wasn't there, "but the best students must make their own way in the world." Her tone was half-compliment and half-insult. Heath and Chardonnay politely ignored it. "This is my son, Heathcliff Claymore."

"Your—oh yes, you mentioned you had—I remember," Chardonnay said by way of greeting. They shook hands. "It is a pleasure to meet you."

"You have me at a disadvantage," Heath replied, hoping he wasn't blushing. "I know nothing of you."

"Never regaled you with stories of her students?"

"There were circumstances," Heath said, running a hand along his sleeve as if to remind Chardonnay of the tattoos.

"Forgive me, there were circumstances, family drama."

"A very fanciful way of putting it," Rainchild said, which was an understatement. "They branded him."

"We don't need to get into that," Heath said.

"Quite right," Chardonnay said. "I should—" looking about. "I came to pay my respects. You have a concert to prepare for."

"Prepare for other guests, more accurately," she replied. "You were just the first."

"Of course," and then he left, leaving Heath alone with his mother.

"Charming," she said, turning, returning to the lounge chairs. "You can stop pretending you do not know him."

"What?"

"Etiquette of the revelries, I know." She sat, motioning for him to take the recently abandoned chair. "Now you have a name and clan to go with the face. Practically a breach of decorum."

"I knew his name," said with a brisk sweep of hand as he accepted the chair.

"Definite breach," leaning back as if she might laugh. "That's why you're here."

"Not why I'm here."

"Not his name, don't be silly. You wanted to know more about him. Figured I would know."

"No." It sounded true. She knew all the reed masters and their students.

"You talked, I'm sure," leaning forward, drawing a breath of slow realization. "You heard him play that foolish music of his."

"It's not foolish—"

"It's foolish," definite, dismissive. "Helps us not at all to control those wretched goats."

"There's more to life than those wretched goats."

"Better to let the world burn, is it? They murdered your father." She meant his step-father, Arturo Claymore. Heath didn't try to correct her. "Burned him alive. Tore him limb from limb." It had been quite the horrifying accident. The goats were remorseless and unforgiving. "How does Chardonnay's foolishness help us with that?"

Heath felt the pain swelling in his chest, building like a bubble that would burst through his heart. He wanted to resist. "I don't"—tripping over words—"know."

"He'll never be a reed master," Lady Rainchild said. Heath tried not to wince. "He'll be a simple musician, playing his silly tunes. His audience may even cheer. Throw him a few coins if he is very lucky."

"He's not the only one," Heath finally managed.

It was his mother's turn to wince as if he had struck her across the face.

"It's not unheard of," she tried to say, "for masters to develop late."

"How late?" he asked.

She was a reed master. She was a great teacher, known far and wide. She had been trying to teach him for years. He watched her struggle to answer.

"Late." The word was a hollow husk of sound.

"Maybe a different approach is called for."

The words stung her. He watched them burrow into her skin. She did not answer.

"Maybe I would be happy," he said.

"Maybe you would," little more than a whisper.

Heath stayed for coffee, sipping a cup slowly, nibbling sandwiches. His mother was quiet. She did not ask how his career among the goat-dung shovelers was progressing, if the days were good or bad. Others did appear, dignitaries from the various clans wanting to meet with the great reed master and teacher. Heath used this as an excuse to leave.

There was a garden. The rooms and suites for the distinguished guests of the goat trials were not properly part of the high coliseum complex, but they did share a secluded garden with passages connecting the two. There were trees. There were benches. There was a fountain. It was pleasantly quiet. The fountain burbled and sang. Birds played at the edge of the water.

Chardonnay Chalice was there, situated on one of the benches so that he could almost discreetly watch the descent from the guest suites. He raised a hand, spying Heath, knowing he had been seen, looking as if he might wave, holding his fingers motionless in the air.

"Clan Amaryllis," Heath said, approaching.

"Clan Melaleuca," Chardonnay replied, rising. They

did not clasp hands in greeting. Their clans were bitter rivals.

"My mother would not have mentioned you," Heath said, teasing.

"Your mother did mention you," also teasing, returning to the bench, reclining upon it like an indulgent demigod.

"I am suitably scandalized," admiring Chardonnay. It was practically a breach of decorum for his mother to have spoken of him to a reed pipe student from another clan.

"I am sincere in my apology," Chardonnay said, sounding sincere. "I should have recognized you before."

"There was no reason for you to have known."

"Lady Rainchild spoke frequently and with great affection of her son, Heathcliff Claymore."

"I am—" Heath said, doubting the words, all but tripping over them. "Honored."

"And I am sorry," sounding quite sincere, "for the blundering, ham-fisted way that I brought up . . . the branding."

"It's all right."

"Lady Rainchild did not speak of this, but I should have recognized," Chardonnay said, as if doubting he should continue, drawing himself upright as if realizing the sprawl across the bench made him look callus and cold. "She once showed me the branding on her own arms." She wore long sleeves—always—to hide the tattoos.

"They are related," Heath said. "Property of the dancing men."

"She did not say—"

"She can't," interrupting, running a hand along his arm as if he might show Chardonnay the marks. "That's part of the branding."

"And you?"

"Different branding. Less summoning. More invocation."

"That the skills of the original reed masters would flow through you?"

Heath took a deep breath like a sigh, remembering being held down and restrained, the tattoos forced upon him while his uncle watched. It had been excruciatingly painful. "That was the idea," he said, "when the original plan for my mother . . . went sideways . . . failed."

"She never—"

"She can't, like I said," interrupting again. "As near as I can piece together." His uncle had told him, taunting, usually while shouting, in broken bits and fragments. "Lady Rainchild was to be the mother of a great reed master. Seed taken directly from the source."

"So to speak," Chardonnay said.

Heath tried to smile, feeling bile in his throat. "So to speak."

The dancing men were mysterious. The dancing men were unknowable. The dancing men had once taught the clans how to tame the fire-breathing goats of death, make and carve the reed pipes from the bones of ancient gods. Nobody knew why.

The dancing men could be summoned. Doing so was dangerous. The dancing men were capricious and unpredictable.

"Lady Rainchild loved," Heath said, speaking slowly as if struggling with a half-remembered monologue, "the wrong one."

"That's . . . unfortunate."

It was more complicated than Heath implied. His mother had been so young—barely thirteen—and had not wanted one of the dancing men to be the father of her child. The secret father had been in defiance of the clan's wishes and something of a desperate choice to keep some small measure of control over her own life. None of which Heath really understood or would have said to Chardonnay, had he known.

"Nobody knows my father," Heath said with the pretense of a bow. "Evidence suggests that he was not a reed master."

"And so, Lady Rainchild lives apart."

"And her son," bowing again, "is a common dung shoveler with markings," indicating his sleeves again, "that many would kill for."

"That is," sounding wistful, "most unfortunate."

Heath sat, flopping onto the bench next to Chardonnay as if he lacked the strength to stand a moment longer. Chardonnay tried to make room for him. It was more love seat than park bench.

"I am a most indifferent student," Heath said. "The goats mock me."

"The goats mock me," Chardonnay countered, commiserating. "Impressed not at all by my attempts at music."

"Everybody's a critic."

"Everybody most certainly is a critic."

"You should teach me."

"What?"

"If I cannot impress the goats, then I would at least attempt music to make the world ache and burn," Heath said, remembering songs drifting through the rafters, feeling them echo beneath his skin.

"I'm little more than a student myself, doing reasonably well in the trials." Chardonnay seemed to consider his own words as if having heard them only after they fled his mouth. "Reasonably well," he muttered. "But I am no teacher."

"And I am no student," which was true.

"The two do not balance out."

"My mother tries. She really does," which was also true. "But it may be the wrong approach. Something I said to her . . . just now," looking back toward the guest suites. "Another approach might be necessary."

"One less focused on controlling the goats? She must have loved hearing that."

"It was just a thought," Heath said with a defeated sigh, feeling the breath slip away into the dust. "It did not go over well."

"I can't imagine that it would have," Chardonnay said.

"Still," Heath said, trying to sound hopeful, "it is a thought."

Chardonnay kept his thoughts to himself.

Secrets

The goat trials ended, as they always did, after the winnowing rounds of competition were completed, the judges' tabulations were posted, and the prizes were handed down. Ash November scored very well and may have even been awarded one of the grand prizes. Heath barely noticed. Celebrations back at the Clan Melaleuca farming complex lasted days. These were harder to ignore.

As the goat trials had ended, the celebrations eventually wound down. The needs and responsibilities of the Clan Melaleuca farming complex began their own slow return to normal. The fire-breathing goats of death demanded care and attention. The flaming-pellet wagons beckoned. Peregrine and Heath did their rounds, making deliveries, collecting empty hot boxes. Heath lost track of the time since he had last held reed pipes in his hands, attempted to practice, tried to play.

Heath had lessons. He had been ignoring them. He had been neglecting his mother, too. They had not spoken since the goat trials.

It was time. His mother may have even sent him a note by way of peace offering, hoping he would return. She had news. The note hinted at the potent potential of news.

Heath took public transportation to his mother's school. He simply wasn't important enough to be allowed to sign out a car. It's possible he could have asked his mother to send him a chauffeured ride, but the thought never crossed his mind. He had the day free. Public transit was fine.

The school was still buzzing from the excitement of the goat trials, time seeming not to have passed for them, enthusiasm driving the students beyond anything resembling talent or ability. Given time, they would learn. Passion and drive were the important part. Skill was talent and training mixed with hard work, heavy emphasis on the hard work.

Heath was shown to rooms by servants. It may have even been the same rooms where he had surrendered his father's reeds. He may have even recognized the servants. He knew so few of them anymore, spending so much time at the farming complex or on his dung-shoveling rounds. He waited nervously, sitting, standing—not wanting to sit—pacing, sitting once more. They had not spoken since the goat trials. The note had been portentous.

His mother swept into the room, summer dress flowing around her, sleeves rustling, enveloping her arms. Heath moved to stand, realizing that he was already standing, continued his attempt to climb into the air anyway.

"Heathcliff, my darling Heathcliff," his mother said, moving toward him in an almighty rush that made him want to back away or run screaming from the room. He backed away. She caught him, squeezed him tightly.

"Mother," he managed to say, arms flailing in the air, unsure whether to embrace her or attempt to pry himself loose.

"It is so good to see you," she said and then kissed him with great gusty passion on the cheek.

"And you," as words otherwise failed him.

"My darling, darling Heathcliff," holding him at arm's length. "I don't know what you said. I do not know what you did, but I thank you."

"I deny everything without hesitation or reservation," he said. "You cannot prove—"

"Cannot prove, my sorry asterisk," interrupting, chiding.

"Mother," trying to pull away, but her hold was strong. "I do not pretend to know—"

"He's coming back," interrupting again.

"He is?" uncertain.

"Coming back," exuberant.

"I fear," finally managing to escape her grasp, "I am lacking critical details in this exchange."

"Chardonnay Chalice," she said. "Remember Chardonnay Chalice? Your friend of the revelries?"

"I remember Chardonnay—"

"He wrote to me," turning, all but dancing across the room. "He wants to come back. Resume his lessons."

"That's," he said, watching her take a letter from a bureau drawer. "Somewhat unexpected."

"You remember our conversation from the goat trials, that's good," she said, holding the letter edgewise to her lips. "You sensed we were not on the best of terms."

"It was hard to miss."

"A difference in philosophies." She crossed the room, holding the letter out to him as if she might let him read it. "Students think they know everything, assert themselves."

"An overabundance of youthful idealism."

"He's wised up." She seemed disappointed Heath had not tried to grab the letter, which was true. She was disappointed. "Aged up. Grown up. Whatever."

"He's coming back."

"Yes, learned his lesson," she said, dancing back across the room. "Accepted the needs—responsibilities—of shepherding the goats. He's not a bad student," stopping again by the bureau. "Quite talented, in fact."

"Just lost his way," Heath said. His mother took a package from one of the drawers. Heath knew at once what it was, even before she began to move with solemn deliberation back toward him.

"By way of *thank you*," she said, holding his father's reeds out to him.

"It hasn't—the suspension," he said, edging away as if the elegantly wrapped bundle would strike him dead.

"Stuff the suspension in a hole among the roots of a milkwood tree. They are my reeds . . . technically," holding the package more firmly out to him. "And I give them to you. My brother need neither know nor care."

"He does care," Heath said, reaching for the reeds with aching caution. "So do I," taking them, unwrapping them quickly, admiring them. "Thank you," he finally said.

"How else did you expect to continue your lessons?" she said. "Come, let us begin."

The lesson did not go well.

"You're out of practice," his mother said but kindly, hiding her ill-formed temper as well as she could.

"I know."

"You need space to practice. The farm," she said, turning words over as if contemplating them. "I don't know. Hard for you to focus there. Bad for concentration."

"They might hear me and confiscate the reeds."

"Exactly," she said, sighing. "If only you might come here."

"Every day?" sounding incredulous. "I'll figure something."

"Stay for supper?" she asked by way of non-sequitur change of subject.

"It's early," he said. "I should go."

He had plans to meet with Ash November but didn't feel the need to share this detail with her. The well-to-do students had private suites and apartments away from the farming complex, where they could gather free from the ferocious oversight of teachers and clan leadership. It was one of the few places where Heath and Ash could spend time together.

"Of course." She knew all about the private suites.

There were parting hugs, kind words, and affectionately polite kisses applied to cheeks.

Magpie Volker was waiting for him by the front door. She had his coat waiting for him. Magpie was Peregrine's mother and had worked for the Claymore family for many years. It was how Heath and Peregrine knew each other. Heath had needed childhood friends because of his unusual, complex, and downright scandalous parentage, and the children of servants served friendship's purpose very well.

"Staying out of trouble?" she asked, offering up the coat.

"I'm trying," said half-mumbled while shrugging into the jacket. His father's reeds went into a pocket, fancy wrappings and all. His fingers lingered over them, and then he realized Magpie was holding a letter.

"A private word," said with mischievous eyes, presenting the letter like an impromptu gift.

"What is it?" Heath asked. Nobody sent him correspondence at his mother's school.

"It's from a former student, recently returned." Mischief had migrated to her voice. "He made it quite clear your mother was not to know."

"Let's try to keep it that way," taking the letter. There was no name. The envelope was blank. It could be from only one person. He wanted so much to rip it open but knew he had to wait. His mother might appear at any moment. "Thank you."

He hugged her, which was unusual but not unheard of. Magpie's daughter was his oldest friend, after all. He departed without additional words.

The walk to the bus stop was excruciating. The wait was impossible. He found a seat toward the back, feeling the bus grumble and groan. He watched his mother's home and school slip into the distance and only then finally tore the letter open.

It was an invitation—directions, times, dates, and places. He had to think. He did not even know if he was on the right bus. His watch told him the day was good and that Chardonnay Chalice would be waiting.

A complex transitioning of buses followed, transferring from one to another, seeking the path that would eventually lead him to the letter's destination. The directions were less clear than Chardonnay had thought they would be and failed to take into account whether Heath would have the city bus schedules and routes memorized.

He arrived at last, deposited at an intersection as far from the Clan Melaleuca farming complex as from his mother's school. There was an old fountain and a bit of a cobblestone square. Water did not so much spring from the fountain's depths as dribble, looking as if it had lost all hope and joy in the wonders of the world. There were café tables scattered haphazardly about, looking as if they had once been spray-painted with rust.

There were people scattered around the tables, ignoring sandwiches wrapped in paper, neglecting small cups of stillborn coffee, and there was music to make Heath's heart ache just to hear it. Chardonnay was on the lowest step of the fountain, practically resting on the cobbled path, and he was playing reed pipes as if he was lost to the world.

Heath listened, wandering among people and tables, crossing to the very edge of the fountain. He stood, wanting to sit, unable to move. The music was the memory of forgotten autumn tasted from the heartless depths of winter dreaming of spring. The song drifted to a close long before the waking sun might return.

Chardonnay noticed him standing before the steps like a gangly tree struggling to understand whatever had happened to its fallen leaves.

"Clan Melaleuca," Chardonnay said, as if sharing a secret.

"Clan Amaryllis," Heath replied, as if confessing a lie.

"I am found out."

"You wanted to be found," looking around. The streets were brick. The buildings were cobbled stone, towering over them like annoyed teachers or angry parents. The people at their tables seemed to be coming to the slow realization that the song had ended and that their coffees had grown cold. "This is returning to the fold?"

"You have spoken with your mother."

"I have—indeed—spoken with my mother, Lady Rainchild."

"It seemed the only way," said with a resigned shrug, "to get a letter to you."

"Steep price for a letter."

"Well," sounding sheepish, stalling for time. "Wasn't just the letter. I realized something after we spoke."

"Oh?"

"The things Lady Rainchild has endured. What you told me. I didn't know."

"Hardly anybody knows."

"Left me feeling selfish, unreasonable."

"I doubt that's true," Heath said. "I mean you're not unreasonable, selfish."

"I know what you meant."

"You were feeling responsible, maybe? To your clan?"

"Something like that."

"They're not mutually exclusive," Heath said. "They shouldn't be, anyway."

"No, they shouldn't," Chardonnay replied. "The judges disagree."

"Oh yes, the goat trials."

"Didn't do as well as I might have hoped," Chardonnay muttered, grumbling. "And it occurred to me—because of our talk—thoughts of responsibility, what others have sacrificed."

"Others have sacrificed." Heath's fingers drifted to his sleeves, feeling the scars even through the fabric.

"It occurred to me that making amends with Lady Rainchild, reaching out to you, would improve my standing with the judges."

"Wait, what?"

"She hasn't been actively poisoning the well, so to speak," Chardonnay said, "but a good word to the judges from one's teacher—"

Heath started to laugh.

"—does wonders," Chardonnay finished, voice wandering, drifting slow. "It's not the only reason."

Heath dropped to the fountain step next to Chardonnay, trying to gain control of himself.

"My dear Amaryllis," Heath said when he could speak. "It never has to be only one reason. Everybody wins." Heath spread his arms wide to take in the surrounding people and tables.

"I did want to see you."

"That you did."

"Lady Rainchild—"

"You have made her happy," interrupting.

"That is good—"

"You have made me happy," placing his arm around Chardonnay's shoulders.

"That is . . . very good."

"This," taking in the crowd again, "is hardly returning to the fold."

"Everybody wins," Chardonnay said, echoing Heath's own words, but meekly.

"As long as my mother does not find out," Heath said. "It might dampen her spirits."

"I would prefer her to be happy."

"So don't tell her."

"Wasn't planning on telling her."

"And we are far, far away from anyone who might do so," taking in their surroundings, savoring the swarthy atmosphere, trickling fountain, rusty tables, rickety chairs and stained cobblestones. "Very far away, indeed."

"All part of the plan," Chardonnay said.

"It's a good plan."

"Not the only place where I might ply my disreputable music."

"No?"

"But one of the few where I might do so publicly," Chardonnay said. "The others are . . . more private . . . fewer ears . . . fewer eyes."

"Somewhere to practice," Heath said. "Where they won't throw vegetables or stones."

"Somewhere," Chardonnay said as if daring himself to speak, "where I could share secrets, tutor and teach."

"Oh really?"

"We would both learn."

"That." Heath put a hand to his face, feeling his breath shake as if he had never considered the possibilities before. "That," said like a needle skipping, threatening to repeat over and over again.

"Or I could give this all up," Chardonnay said, taking in the fountain, small assortment of tables and chairs. "Be the good little reed-master goatherd."

"Oh no, don't do that."

"Then you would learn?" drawing in his breath as if expecting Heath to answer but failing to give adequate time for a response to form. "It would be good for both of us."

"Yes, you said."

"It would help me form and refine my ideas, the shape of the music. All in my head right now, making sense only to me."

"And I would benefit from a different approach," Heath said, knowing he was repeating himself, echoing words spoken during the goat trials. "Might actually improve or something," thinking of the day's miserable session with his mother.

"Everybody wins," Chardonnay said, taking in the world around them.

"Everybody wins," Heath echoed with a sly smile.

"But not here," said as if surprising himself. "Here is too open for introductory lessons."

"Agreed."

"We'll have to meet—the letter, you have the letter?"

"I have the letter."

"Follow the letter," Chardonnay said, as if trying to hold onto the quiet center of his soul. "We'll meet. Find places where we might practice together in private."

"I'll follow the letter."

"I should," looking about. The audience was growing restless at the lack of music. "I'm not done . . . here. You should stay," indicating an open table where small birds contemplated the crumbs of a forgotten sandwich. "Listen."

"I should," Heath said, looking past the tables. "Go . . . I have errands," meaning he was supposed to be meeting Ash November.

"First lesson," raising a solitary finger.

"I have . . . appointments. It's late, and the buses are such a long way from here."

"I can take you."

"Oh no, that's not a good idea."

"It's no bother."

"Clan Amaryllis," said reluctantly.

Chardonnay caught at his breath as if trying to stop an inopportune remark, swallowed slowly. They were from rival clans. "Clan Melaleuca," he finally said.

Heath stood but slowly, patting Chardonnay on the shoulder as he climbed. Chardonnay reached up as if he would stop Heath, letting their fingers play together before finally letting go.

It was a sprawling city. Nobody thought about how large. Technically, the city was several small towns, the edges having blurred together, the names having faded until they were nothing more than ink on a map. All anybody remembered was the grand metropolis. Nobody considered how long it took to get anywhere until they needed public transportation.

For example, it was more bus rides than Heath wanted to count before he found himself back in proper Clan Melaleuca territory. The reed-pipe-student private apartments were a discreet distance from the clan's farming complex. Heath was very late—bitter twilight—streetlights slowly burning.

He found the door, row of buttons, pressed the buzzer. It was more a suite of apartments mixed and linked together than individual living spaces, resembling the shared accommodations of the farming complex. There was a great common loft, open space like a factory floor with a vaulted ceiling. There were rooms that were little more than sitting rooms or sleeping quarters branching off of it. There were more complete suites, like little apartments all to themselves.

It was a grand menagerie that the Clan Melaleuca reed-pipe students had been using with varying degrees of clan leadership's knowledge and approval for years. Heath knew the space well if only someone— anyone—would answer the door. He had been leaning on the buzzer for ages.

There was movement beyond the door at last, Heath could tell, and he finally released the buzzer. The door opened, and he pushed past Dandelion Hatfield-Volker.

"I'm sorry," Heath rattled off quickly, feeling as if he should rush the stairs. "I'm late. I'm very late. I'll make it up to you."

"He's not here," Dandelion said. Health almost crashed into the wall, feeling as if he had been caught on a hook. "Ash November went out."

"No," pleading through sure force of will for it not to be true.

"He couldn't wait, I fear." Dandelion was the caretaker of the private suites and knew all of their secrets. Heath and Dandelion were even fairly good friends. "He didn't leave a message."

"I couldn't," Heath said, stumbling over words, pressing fingers to his face. Nobody considered the city sprawling or transit underfunded. "I couldn't get away—I'm sorry."

"He knows," Dandelion said. "I'm sure he knows. I will tell him that you were unavoidably delayed." Dandelion still had the door half-open. Heath knew he couldn't stay.

"Do you know where?"

Dandelion gave him a look as if judging whether to point out he had been specifically told not to let him know. Heath held his breath, knowing the question was an imposition.

"Drinking, I think," Dandelion finally said. "Ash November. Cassandra Laughingstock. Some of the other high-octane students."

"The goat trial prize winners."

"They needed the distraction, I fear. There was some excitement today, but I'm sure you are well aware."

"No, I don't," Heath said. "It was my free day. I had lessons—saw my mother."

"There was a rogue goat—"

"No."

"—several houses destroyed—in our territory—burned to the ground." Dandelion sounded scandalized. "A young goat—little more than a kid—like that last time before the goat trials."

"Another rogue kid?" Heath felt numb. He remembered the smoke. He could taste the flames. The goat had studied him with indifferently evil eyes. "That's wondrous strange."

"Ash, Cassandra, the others, they were worked up—everyone."

"No, of course," Heath said. "I should have been there," stumbling over words, feeling absurd hearing them. "I should have—I don't know—I don't understand."

"You should go home, Heathcliff. It's late."

Heath looked up from his toes, realized that he had been staring at his toes, studied Dandelion's face. It was late, and the door still stood half-open.

Heath nodded his head, weakly, defeated. He made his way back to the bus stop and slowly found his way home. The city sprawled around him, an indifferent abyss.

Complications

It was several weeks before Heath could make his way back to the broken square, café seating, and disheveled fountain. The needs of the flaming-pellet wagon had kept him far too busy, lessons with his mother having burned away even more of his time. Chardonnay never performed for the fountain crowds on a reliable schedule, which hadn't helped. Heath had finally resorted to sending notes via Magpie Volker.

Heath stood among the café tables at last, public transit having dumped him in the general vicinity of reed-pipe music, cobbled streets, and lovesick fountain. Chardonnay was winding down the show, Heath's duties having prevented him from attending more of the performance.

"At last," Chardonnay said, wrapping and putting away his reeds. "Clan Melaleuca."

"Finally," Heath said. "Clan Amaryllis."

"It was not intended to be such a game."

"Magpie was amused," which was true. "Makes all the bother worthwhile."

"Magpie—oh yes, the go-between," Chardonnay said. "It did seem to make her extraordinarily happy."

"All that matters," Heath said, ignoring the fact Chardonnay had not bothered to learn her name.

"Shall we go? I have a ride," waving to one of the tables. There was a young man. There were several cups of what had once been coffee, and there were two young women quickly realizing they were no longer the center of the young man's attention.

"Oh, I had not considered," Heath said, watching him cautiously.

"How else did you think we were going to reach more familial climes?" Chardonnay said, standing, walking to the table. "Arabesque," patting the young man on the shoulder, turning back toward Heath, "this is Heathcliff."

"Clan Melaleuca," Arabesque said.

"Yes, well, we all know who did what," Chardonnay said. "My cousin can be charming," said in Heath's general direction, meaning Arabesque. "When he's not busy trying to protect me from unwanted influences."

"We all have influences," Heath said, pacing slowly, feeling like a caged tiger. "Clan Amaryllis," said directly at Chardonnay's cousin.

Arabesque made a sound like the dismissive snort a rhinoceros might make. "Ride's this way," he said, turning, starting to walk.

"Best we'll get out of him," Chardonnay said, trying to sound upbeat, trying not to look worried, watching Heath. "Coming?"

It was a bit of a walk to the car, which turned out to be a little two-seat spitfire that could technically fit a third person in back. Heath managed it. Arabesque drove frighteningly fast.

"Lessons continue?" Chardonnay said, twisted half-way around so that he was almost facing the back. Heath could barely understand him.

"Yes." Heath shouted to be heard. The fancy sports car was fast and loud. "They progress, I suppose."

"We'll see what we can do about that. Surprise your mother, maybe?"

"She'll love that," he said. "What about you? Lessons, right?"

"They progress." Chardonnay tried to smile. "Lady Rainchild is the best teacher I have ever known. It's quite a thing that I am allowed to study with her."

"Clan Amaryllis."

"Clan Amaryllis, indeed," Chardonnay said. Their clans really did hate each other. "I have to be careful. Not drag my ideas about performance and composition into the equation."

"You'll have another falling out," Heath said. "Can't have that."

"Cannot have that," sounding thoughtful. "Quite a thing that I can study with her," sounding wistfully remorseful. "Speaking of the intricacies of clan politics and warfare, it won't be as easy as I thought to get you into my private suites."

"I'm used to it." Heath tried an indifferent shrug, which turned out to be nearly impossible while wedged into the back of the car. "Reed students and their private spaces."

"But you are a reed-pipe student."

"Not a very good one, I told you," Heath said, failing another shrug. "Officially, I'm not. Most of them don't even know my mother gives me lessons."

"What do you do then?" Chardonnay asked. "Officially."

Heath took a deep breath as if he might bite through the words, not wanting to speak them.

"I work the flaming-pellet wagons," said with a sigh.

"You're a dung shoveler?" Arabesque said. The question shouted like an explosive laugh.

"Be nice," Chardonnay said.

"I was set to be part of the reed chorus," Heath said, sounding desperate, sounding like he was pleading even to his own ears. "At the goat trials."

"That would have been something."

"That fell through." There was no reaction from the front seat. "So do I have to wear a bag over my head?"

"It won't come to that," Chardonnay said. "People are on edge. The rogue goat. We'll have to be careful."

"The rogue goat," Heath said, remembering the fire, remembering contempt and insanity for eyes. "All anyone can talk about."

"What is it now? Two? Three?"

"Three," Arabesque said.

"Only two," Heath corrected him. "One before the goat trials. We all thought it was related to the goat trials. Some group or other. One after the trials."

"Easy to explain away one before the trials," Chardonnay agreed. "Some group or other trying to show what could be done with a young goat. Snipe business. Gain financing. Went explosively wrong."

"I was there," Heath said. "Very explosively wrong."

"You were there?"

"Dung shoveler, remember? Rogue goat was on my rounds. What a coincidence," sounding absurd even as he said it.

"That must have been something."

"Why I was cut from the chorus," Heath said, the memory burning. "Reeds confiscated." Took a slow breath. Eyes closed. "Because I tried to quiet the goat."

"You stood up to a rogue goat?" Arabesque sounded shocked.

"It was only a kid."

"Well, if that's all. Make it sound easy, why don't you." Arabesque still sounded impressed.

"It wasn't—yeah, it wasn't," Heath said. "Confiscated my reeds . . . confiscated—only just got them back."

"So, what I'm hearing is that you are out of practice," Chardonnay said, trying to sound light as if noticing that Heath was burned by the memory.

"I'm not a very good student."

"Well, we shall see what we can do about that."

They arrived, old part of town, white stone and red brick-lined streets. Rows of houses pressed edge to edge as if they were secretly one very long lodging, the individual front doors acting as little more than a disguise to throw off the unsuspecting passersby. Very narrow alleyway around back was barely wide enough to fit the little sports car. The way dipped underground, opening up into an extensive garage that served all the houses above. Everything was brick and stone, as if the architects had been determined to stick with the theme.

They climbed cobbled steps, moving carefully as if expecting random people to jump out at them at any moment. They opened one door with a tiny key, and the stairs switched to uneven, warped, and well-worn wood that creaked mightily at the slightest touch.

They passed common rooms, everything small. There was a bit of a lounge. There was a tiny library. There was another sitting room or possibly another library. Books were everywhere.

They reached one final door. Another key was applied, and they stood at last in a small parlor, table and chairs. Somewhere beyond was another room with maybe a couch. It was hard to tell.

Chardonnay and Arabesque shared a look.

"I'll be off then," Arabesque said, and he pocketed the key, leaving Chardonnay and Heath alone in the room.

"It's charming," Heath finally said, crossing to the table, realizing the floor sloped ever so slightly toward the door.

"Don't pass judgment all in one go," Chardonnay said. "Lot of history here. Been in the family for generations."

"And that's saying something, I know. The flaming

goats make it hard to keep anything for generations." The table was strewn with manuscripts and music paper. Everything was covered in scribbled notes and jotted notation. "We're all just so flammable."

"Explains the obsession with the reeds." Chardonnay took reed pipes from his satchel, began to unwrap them.

"Doesn't explain our obsession," Heath said, unslinging his own reeds, held them wrapped in soft cloth and leather, held them as if he could not believe they had been returned. "Control."

"It's not all about control," Chardonnay said, sounding wistful. "Well, that's a lot to do with it. Everything being just so flammable, like you said."

"What? Absence makes the heart grow fonder, does it?"

"I doubt that's what I meant." Chardonnay straddled a chair, dumped his reeds onto the table as if they were unimportant or indestructible, not caring which. "Now," he said, motioning to Heath. "Scales."

"I'm out of practice," Heath mumbled, unwrapping. Chardonnay said nothing, only watching him intently, so Heath put the reed pipes to his lips, played a scale. There was no comment from the gallery. Heath sighed, played another.

"Okay, stop," Chardonnay finally said. "You're trying too hard."

"Out of practice," muttered softly.

"You're not sucking a straw, drinking a really thick milkshake. You need . . ." His voice drifted.

"You don't suck on reeds, anyway," Heath said into the silence.

"You do. It's both," Chardonnay countered. "Coming and going, sucking and blowing, it's where harmonics and complex intonations come from. You have a new bedfellow," Chardonnay said and then froze. "You have a—"

"I have a bedfellow, yes," Heath interrupted but quietly.

"Remember when you were young, the relationship fresh, it's your first time going to play a new reed." Chardonnay stopped, laughing at the look on Heath's face. "That's right, you've only had one teacher, and it's your mother."

"It is my mother."

"I'm guessing she stayed away from certain analogies—"

"Yes," Heath said, cutting into Chardonnay's words.

Chardonnay covered his face, trying not to laugh. "But they're so useful," he finally said between fingers.

"I'm still trying to work out the whole sucking and blowing thing," Heath said. "You don't blow your bedfellow's reed . . . bedfellow has to have a reed."

"Well, not the way you mean, anyway. You want to focus air through the reeds like it is an extension of your breathing. Lady Rainchild covered that, yes?"

"Yes."

"Right, so." Chardonnay came around the table, stood next to Heath, and held his own reeds to his lips. "Okay, baby steps, try watching me for a second." He played a simple scale.

Heath lifted his reeds, tried to imitate Chardonnay. The scale was repeated, slower, and Heath tried to copy him.

"Slower," Chardonnay said around his reeds. "Softer."

Health felt his fingers tremble, his lips quivering as if they were about to spasm or tighten into a knot. His mouth burned as if he had bitten into a hot coal or smeared a remnant of flaming-goat dung across his face. He put the reed pipes down, wanting to throw them across the room, hoping they would shatter into millions of tiny shards. Sinking to the floor—a chair would have taken too much effort—he dropped his head into his hands. This made his back ache. His hands wouldn't stop shaking. His face burned even more.

Chardonnay was silent, letting the moment drift while Heath tried not to breathe. "This is progress," Chardonnay finally said.

"It is?" The words a quarrelsome, dubious statement.

"Anger, right? Wanted to throw the reeds across the room?"

Heath gave him a look, biting through his teeth, words failing.

"Means you felt something," Chardonnay said. "Shows you care. Hard part is moving past the anger. Feeling more emotions. Finding more feelings. Letting them flow."

"Not what *they*"—feeling the word burn—"focus on."

"Because of the need to control." Chardonnay moved one of the chairs, sat so that he wasn't towering over Heath. "It limits the range, emphasizing precision."

Chardonnay wandered from view. With his head in his hands, Heath's view had been little more than Chardonnay's feet. Heath felt his whole body ache, feeling the need to groan like an ancient tree twisting in the wind. Chardonnay's feet returned. A water bottle was lowered into his field of view.

Heath took it. His mouth burned. He took a swig, letting the water linger on his tongue.

"It's easy to get caught up in precision, specialization," Chardonnay said. "Refining the thing over and over, whittling down until there's nothing left. So easy to forget why you started."

"Your analogy needs work," Heath said.

"We'll save that for an advanced lesson. On your feet."

Heath rose unsteadily, feeling he would never be able to hold still, and then he picked up his reeds.

"Scales." Chardonnay already had his reed pipes to his lips and began to play.

Heath sighed, a big heavy rumbling of sound that felt like it would send him tumbling back to the floor, and then he tried to follow, catch up with Chardonnay mid-note.

There were scales, simple and straightforward. There was movement, growing complex, backward and forward, jumping notes, skipping intervals, octaves, and then jumping keys. There were patterns, follow the leader, and then Heath realized that they had left scales and exercises behind. There was a tune, repeating melody, and then he realized it was a canon. Heath dropped back, holding a note, trilling it, letting Chardonnay move on, and then he picked up the canon, melody harmonizing with itself. It was a dance, teasing, flirting with itself.

Heath looked at Chardonnay, studying his fingers, listening to him, remembering the notes so that he could catch them. Chardonnay looked back, his eyes twinkling, delighted.

Chardonnay stopped at last, letting the song fade into silence. He said nothing, glancing away, looking awkward and shy. Heath drifted to a stop. The last note was a muffled squawk like the distant harrumph of a disgusted goose.

"Good," Chardonnay said.

Heath laughed, wanting to bounce up and down.

His heart ached. His face burned. He reached for Chardonnay, moving to kiss him.

"Whoa." Chardonnay stepped back, holding up the reed pipes like a shield.

"Oh." Heath floundered over words.

"The revelries are over," Chardonnay said, stepping away, letting the space grow between them.

"Right, sorry, I didn't . . . think," Heath mumbled, studying the floor. His face suddenly burning and sloppy with tears. "Sorry."

"Quite all right, no sorry." Chardonnay was halfway round the table, holding the distance. "It's the rush. Happens all the time."

"Yes, right, probably why I was looking forward to the reed chorus," and then he started to laugh, wondering if he would ever stop.

"This is why having a bedfellow is good."

"Yes—oh god, I'm so sorry," wiping at his face.

"It's fine," Chardonnay said. "Probably enough lessons for one night."

"Yes, enough for a first time," started to laugh again. "Should probably remember where I left that bedfellow."

"Good idea."

"Should I—" looking around, desperate. "I should go."

"Yes, but there's no need to rush." Chardonnay sat, the first chair he had straddled on the far side of the table facing Heath. "I want you to come back. Sit," indicating the chairs on Heath's side. "Drink," indicating the neglected water bottle.

"No need to run." Heath took the closest chair. "I want to come back."

"Tell me about your bedfellow, if you don't mind," Chardonnay said, conversationally, inviting. "Doubt I know them."

"You might. He scored very well at the goat trials. May have even gotten a prize."

"You don't know?"

"I've had other things on my mind," kicking himself for not having bothered to find out in all the weeks since the trials ended. "Wasn't the most pleasant of times—the chorus."

"Of course."

"Ash November—"

"Ash November?" interrupting, all but speaking over Heath. "He's—"

"I know."

"Scored very well—"

"I figured."

Chardonnay drew breath to speak, shout more staccato sentence fragments, but caught himself, choking on the words. A minor coughing fit followed. Chardonnay tried to shove his fist into his mouth.

"Future reed master, clan leader," Heath said and then made a great show of shrugging his shoulders as if defying the fates to shout insults. "Dung shoveler," indicating himself.

"How did you manage that?"

Heath tried—failed—not to flinch.

"My mother is a great teacher," he finally said. "It's an honor to study with her," was as close to an explanation as Heath wanted to give.

Chardonnay said nothing, looking dumbfounded, the table between them. Heath had met Ash at his mother's school. The future clan leader had been exploring, feeling entitled. They had met. Heath stayed at his mother's house at various times for various reasons. Ash had found him in a spare room, changing. They had hit it off rather quickly.

"I have led a rich but sheltered life," Chardonnay muttered, sounding wistful.

"I should go," Heath said, realizing that he didn't know where he was. "I don't know how I'm going to get home."

"Arabesque can take you," Chardonnay said. "Or I can drive," he hurriedly added, catching Heath's look.

They escaped the building, winding stairs, tiptoeing like thieves to avoid drawing anyone's attention. The little two-seater called to them. Chardonnay drove. Heath gave directions once they were back in parts of the city that he recognized.

Heath had Chardonnay drop him at the bus stop several blocks from the Clan Melaleuca reed-pipe students' private flats. Rival clans spotting each other even from a distance was still a concern that he did not need to explain to his impromptu driver. Chardonnay did not wait. The walk did him good. He didn't even have to lean on the door buzzer for long. Ash opened the door himself.

"Hey," Heath said breathlessly, surprised, before Ash could get a word out.

"Hey yourself," Ash said, holding the door, making room for him. Ash looked hastily dressed, as if he had noticed Heath dithering before the door—just happened to glance at the lobby camera at the right moment—and Heath realized he must look a puzzled fright. "This is—" Ash started to say.

"Unexpected, I know, I'm sorry," interrupting. "I just—I had to," and then he hiccupped, quivering, shaking, feeling like he would degenerate into laughter or thunderous sobbing at any moment.

"Hey—no sorry," Ash said, abandoning the door, reaching for him. Door slid silently closed. "Always welcome—damn them," taking in the assembled apartments, meaning the other reed-pipe students who might look down at him.

"Can we—before I make a scene or give your comrades more gossip?"

"Of course."

They climbed stairs. There was an elevator, but they climbed stairs. Fewer people used the stairs. They stopped before Ash's door, his hand resting on the handle.

"So . . . um, company," Ash said before turning the handle.

"Oh," Heath managed before the door was open, and he could see into Ash's private suite.

There was a bit of a sunken living room with couches, soft chairs, coffee table designed to be eaten around with everyone sitting cross-legged on fur rugs. There were steps up to a sleeping area and down to a den. There was a kitchenette off to one side, and a bathroom somewhere off to another.

There was food spread on the coffee table, looking like steamed dumplings, tarts, and savory pastries. There were twin champagne flutes, an open bottle, and Cassandra Laughingstock not wearing much of anything, maybe wrapped in a long silky scarf.

"Oh," she said, putting down the sweet bun she had been slowly crumbling to pieces as something to do while Ash was away.

"I'll find another glass," Ash said into the silence that followed. "Are you hungry?" he asked, indicating the table before disappearing into the kitchenette.

"I don't . . . I don't know," Heath said, realizing he hadn't eaten in hours and was suddenly feeling equal parts famished and as if he never wanted to touch another bite for as long as he lived.

"Well, there's plenty," Cassandra said, looking resigned to the spectacular wreck that had just become her evening. "Come here and admire the possibilities. They're quite good."

"Yes, I'm sure," said staggering over to the table, staring down at the offerings. Heath didn't know if he could find a way to sit that didn't involve him tumbling to the floor. "Yes, it is quite—I've had this before."

"Yes, that explains a lot," Cassandra said. "Things are suddenly making a lot more sense," said in Ash's direction as he bounded back into the living room.

"Be nice," he said, handing Heath the glass, grabbing the bottle, pouring champagne into it. "And sit," directed at Heath.

"Thank you," Heath managed to say without crumbling to the ground. Ash only had to help him a little to settle onto the furs.

"Should I lie and say this is a pleasant diversion?" Cassandra asked.

"You're not actually a snob, Cassie, so you can stop acting like one. There's nobody else around," Ash said, glaring daggers at her.

Cassandra lifted her glass, studied it as if contemplating the depths of her soul. "True," she said, and took a sip. "How are you anyway?" she asked, meaning Heath. "You look a fright."

"I do?" was all Heath could manage, hating how he must look to them.

"Yes."

"You do look as if you've had quite the day," Ash said.

"I don't . . . know," Heath said, eyeing Cassandra.

"It's fine," Ash said. "Public faces, private confidantes. If I didn't think Cassie could be trusted, I would have kicked her out already."

"Ignore me," she offered.

It was true that the responsibilities of clan leadership meant Ash's life was far more complicated than Heath could attempt to follow, and he never tried. He knew Ash would always need to include and be involved with other people, and that some of them could be trusted. It didn't necessarily make things easier.

"I'm sorry, I'm interrupting," Heath said, moving to stand.

"You're not," Ash said.

"Well," Cassandra drew the word out. Heath winced.

"You're not," Ash said more forcefully, directing his voice like a command at Cassandra. She shrugged her shoulders, took another sip, and did not reply.

Silence drifted. Heath realized they were both watching him and felt anything resembling coherent thought run screaming into the depths of night, leaving him without words or a voice to speak them. The moment continued to drift, and he felt panic reach down his throat and strangle his heart.

"I am hungry," he finally managed, a broken fragment of words, each syllable feeling like a stone monolith taking all his strength to lift into the sky.

"We'll start with that," Ash said, hand motions intent on reminding Heath that he held a glass.

The champagne was quite good, Heath had to admit. The food was excellent. There was quiet conversational patter that he couldn't quite follow. Eventually, he laughed at a joke. There was more conversation. It was more lively. Salacious stories and other clan gossip may have even been shared. Laughter flowed.

A new bottle was opened, wine, something exotic and very dark red. Music was put on, also exotic, a singer from faraway lands. It was very pleasant and had nothing to do with pacifying or controlling goats, which was greatly appreciated all around.

"That's what we need," may have been spoken at some point. "More music for its own sake." This may have been met with raucous agreement but otherwise ignored.

They left food uneaten. There had been a surprising quantity, considering it had originally only been meant for two. They left dishes on the coffee table, glasses too, as if they expected mysteriously unseen individuals to clean up while they were not looking, and they decamped for the raised sleeping area.

Clothes started to disappear before they had finished climbing the steps. Cassandra had very little to lose. The bed was large.

There was kissing, stroking, caressing, and touching, Cassandra in the middle. The bed was very soft and comfortable. Arms moving, legs entwined, Ash and Cassandra facing each other, kissing. Heath watched Ash over Cassandra's shoulder, running fingers down her arm and hip, running up over Ash's side.

Ash and Cassandra locked together, moving together, thrusting. Ash's hand moving over her, touching Heath, reaching down, holding, stroking him. Heath gripping Ash's back, moving his hips slowly in time with Cassandra so that Ash's hand could be still, only needing to hold gently.

Heath moaned, turning, cupping his hands. Ash and Cassandra remained locked together. They turned, shifting so that they could both reach for Heath. Their hands stroking his arms, chest.

Ash cried out, moving quickly, jerkily, and then held still. Cassandra ran her hands over him, shoulder, arms, hips and back. They lay together quietly, nobody saying anything for a long time.

There were towels discreetly hidden beside the bed. Heath noticed they were softly scented as he applied one to his fingers and hands, and then he passed a towel to Ash. Cassandra dabbed at her face with another. Nobody thought to say anything.

Eventually, there were discreet trips to the bathroom, ending back at the bed. They stayed snuggled together. There may have even been more activity. Finally, there was sleep.

Exasperations

Heath woke slowly, the sound of soft buzzing surrounding him, lifting him gently—warm and fuzzy—drifting almost leisurely away from dreams and into the waking world. It took him a moment to realize that he had only Cassandra for company. Ash was gone. The buzzing came muffled from Cassandra's hands, held tight between her legs. She was trying to hold still, failing, moving, suddenly shifting in waves that ran the length of her body.

"Good morning," he said but quietly.

"Morning," more surprised gasp than word.

"We seem to be missing someone."

"He was called away," Cassandra said, turning, twisting more than turning. Her hands remained where they were, keeping busy, fingers moving. "Affairs of clan leadership."

"Burdens of responsibility," Heath said, raising a hand, moving it through the air inches from her body as if pretending to stroke her. "It was kind of you to stay."

"Wanted to make sure you were okay," she said, grabbed his hand, pulled it down to join her own. The stone she held was the size of a large egg, warm, and vibrated quite vigorously between their fingers.

"Very kind," fingers moving, slipping around.

"I'm not heartless," she said. "Image to uphold in public, as they say."

Heath turned toward her. She raised her leg, inviting, stroking, caressing with her foot, running it down his leg. He shifted against her, already responding. She only had to reposition the stone a little.

"Responsibilities of your own to uphold," he said.

"Exactly."

They kissed, slow, long, as if they expected to die, letting their bodies move slowly, gently, locked together. His hand drifted across her chest, resting, cupping.

They were quiet, moving together, breathing slow as if trying to preserve a favored dream. She was warm. Her eyes were kind. He tried to smile, kissed her instead. She responded, as if they were old lovers meeting again after years apart.

Heath turned, shifting around. Her legs moved, enveloping him, cupping around his back. Looking down, he lowered his face so that they were nose to nose. There were only her eyes. There were only his.

"Faster," she whispered, barely a breath to brush his lips. He responded, slowly, the tempo quickening like a song gaining momentum, tempting the dancers. "Yes, like that," another whisper.

"Like that," he whispered back to her, moving faster, a quick two-step beat, his heart racing, and then he couldn't see her any more, crying out, more moan than cry. His body shook, buried his face in her shoulder. Her arms were around him, cupping the back of his head, stroking his hair.

He couldn't hold still, warmth taking him. He shivered and moaned, couldn't open his eyes, wanting to bite her shoulder, fill his mouth, muffle his voice. He stopped quaking at last, waves like the sea finally receding. Her arms locked around him, holding him tight. Breathing hard, they were both breathing like exhausted lovers.

They held together, holding still for a long moment lost to time, and then he slid to the side, her arms letting him drift sideways. They lay side by side, Heath studying the ceiling, Cassandra studying him, and then she realized the stone was still buzzing somewhere, lost among the disheveled covers. She rose on one shoulder, found the disquieted thing, silenced it, turned back to him, let a slow breath rise and fall in her chest.

"You're in pain," she finally said, freezing him like a small cat caught by a car's sudden high beams. "You don't feel you can tell him," meaning Ash. "You can tell me. We're not lovers."

He tried to smile.

"You know what I mean," she said.

"I know," barely a whisper of sound.

"Tell me, I won't breathe a word." She touched his shoulder playfully, pressing one finger against him.

Heath cracked his lips as if preparing to make a sound, but nothing came.

"He cares about you, I can tell," she said. "It's been aching at him. I didn't know what. I didn't know why. Now, I do."

"Reed masters and dung shovelers don't mix," he managed.

"That only explains why he wouldn't tell me. Tells me nothing about what's bothering you."

Heath closed his eyes, hand covering his face. She slapped at his fingers, gently but firmly.

"I care about him," she said. "I want him to be a good leader. I want him to be happy, good for my career." He looked at her from between fingers. She tried to smile. "It's not all about me."

Heath looked back at the ceiling, hand drifting to his chest.

"If you're good." She tapped his temple. "He's good."

"I was going to be in the reed chorus," he said, the statement draining away all his words.

"Yeah, I know."

He turned, looking at her, surprised. It was her turn to study the ceiling.

"We keep an eye on the chorus," she said to the semi-dark room. "The more serious future reed masters among us. I remember your audition," without looking at him.

"They didn't want me in the chorus, my uncle, his uncle. They couldn't stop me. I gave them an excuse."

"They were never going to let you perform," studying the ceiling. "They were going to find an excuse even if they had to manufacture one."

"Dung shoveler," he said, grinding words.

"No," she said, turning, touching his face. "I remember your audition."

Heath couldn't breathe, feeling his heart shudder cold, and then he struck at her hand, wanting to tumble from the bed. She let him turn and then rested fingers gently on his arm.

"They let you in because of Ash, Lady Rainchild, but it was always going to be something."

He sat up, dangling over the edge of the bed.

"We should," he said, facing the wall, "clean up."

When she didn't say anything, he stood, staggered slowly to the shower, used it, letting the water run. When he emerged, she was standing on the cold tile, waiting for her turn.

"I know that's not what's bothering you," she said but softly. He froze, watching her. "You can tell me. It doesn't have to be now."

Heath closed his eyes, nodded, and then he left her the shower. She used it. He could hear it running.

He made coffee, toast—the kitchenette had its uses—sat on a tall stool, sipping coffee, nibbling toast. She emerged eventually, appeared genuinely surprised to find he hadn't run away. Cassandra accepted a cup, sat on the next stool.

"I'm taking lessons," Heath said.

"I know," she replied, holding the cup to her lips. "Lady Rainchild."

"No."

She almost did a spit take. "No?" said with her head on one side, more word than question.

"Clan Amaryllis."

Cassandra looked as if she might choke on nothing more than the air in her lungs, and then her whole body shook, coughing fit. Heath took her cup before she could drop it, and she stood, almost doubling over from the pain in her chest. Finally under control, she turned, breathing ragged.

"You're really testing my promise of confidentiality," she said, her voice hoarse, sounding more than a little cross.

"I know."

"Well," she said, struggling to find her seat, fingers seeking as if she could not see. "This explains a lot."

"Does it?"

"There's more?" failing to hide her look of horror.

"Yes, there's more. He's on the outs with his clan—well, I don't actually know—I suspect based on things he's said. He's been on the outs with my mother, that's for sure."

"Wait," Cassandra said, holding a hand flat like a stop sign. "It's not Chardonnay Chalice, is it?"

"You've heard of him?"

"Oh my dear God," bringing her arms around, slamming them together, burying her face in her wrists.

"But he's Clan Amaryllis," bewildered.

"I know he's Clan Amaryllis," Cassandra said from behind her hands, as if trying desperately not to scream. "He's competition. We always keep an eye on the goat trial competition."

"So he's good—you've met him."

"He was good," she said, arms falling. "He's . . . trouble—I don't like that you're taking lessons. He's developed *ideas*," last word less spoken than sneered.

"I am learning," Heath said, countering. "Maybe for the first time, I am actually learning."

"He's a winter snowflake. The goats will melt him down to slush," sneering again. "So much for his ideas."

"The unspoken promise of the whole *you can confide in me* thing is the nonjudgmental part, you know."

Cassandra drew breath deep, face contorting as if she was in actual pain, and for a moment, she looked as if she might cry.

"That's actually true," she said, muttering, the breath slipping from her. A hand drifted toward him, rested on his shoulder, squeezed gently, drifted away. "I am sorry."

"The change in approach is good for me, I think," Heath said. "Even my mother agrees."

"Does she?" looking surprised but trying to cover it because of the nonjudgmental promise. "That's . . . good. If it works for you, that's good."

"It's been a lot," he said, feeling guilty for saying his mother approved. She had said nothing of the kind, but Cassandra had been so quietly and condescendingly judgmental of Chardonnay's ideas.

"I'm sure," she replied, gripping his arm, attempt at comforting. "It's been a lot for me this morning," attempting a smile.

"You did ask."

"I did ask."

"I should—" turning, looking about. "What time is it?"

"Ash said you have a free day."

"He's tracking my schedule?"

"He's a future clan leader," she said, as if stating the obvious. "And he cares about you," which was less obvious but very true.

"I should still—" slipping from the stool, standing. "Thank you," he said.

"He cares about you. Helping you makes him a better leader." She grabbed his arm as he moved to leave the kitchenette. "I want you to tell me how things go with your Clan Amaryllis lessons."

"I don't—"

"He cannot know," interrupting. "He cares about you, and he cannot know."

"I know," Heath said quietly. The cross-clan scandal could damage Ash's career, his leadership. Plausible deniability might become important.

Heath gathered his things, Cassandra watching him from her perch in the kitchenette. He left Ash's private suite, closing the door, walking away. He imagined Cassandra screaming wild obscenities at the empty ceiling now that he was gone, which she was. The soundproofing was good.

He thought about walking back to the farming complex. It wasn't that far, and the buses were starting to feel like a nuisance, spending so much time on them. The neighborhood was nice. The favored reed-pipe students liked living well. There were fancy shops taking space at street level in all the buildings. Many of them spilled onto the sidewalk, offering food, clothing, or crafts, all tactfully displayed.

Heath had been walking for a while, just soaking in his surroundings, when it finally started to register that the clan farming complex and reed-pipe student private abodes were farther apart than memory wanted him to believe. He tried to identify the closest public transportation lines, which took some small amount of doing. He was almost, but not quite, lost.

Some intricate distribution and navigation of transit options deposited him at the clan complex and home at last. The shared apartments and communal living space were navigated. Peregrine was on the couch, facing the television, console gaming with great focus and intensity. It was some combination of side-scrolling and hand-to-hand-fighting, single player.

"Hey," Peregrine said matter-of-factly without looking away from the screen.

The other flatmates appeared to be nowhere in the vicinity, which wasn't really a surprise. Off days were staggered for a reason and helped reduce the chances they would murder each other in fits of drunken rage.

Heath disappeared into the communal bathroom, took another shower. It had been a warm day, and he had walked more than he had realized, the city's scale being a true blind spot to its inhabitants. When Heath emerged in fresh clothes, Peregrine had not moved. This was not a surprise.

He plopped himself on the couch next to her, watched the screen for some small puddle of time.

"Is this a new one?" he asked. "I don't recognize the level."

"Nope," she replied, eyes focused, fingers flying. "Revelation Anarchy, level nine. You're just no good at this one."

"True." He watched for a while. "Let me try," reaching for the controller.

"Hey, let me save first," trying to hold the controller out of reach while trying desperately not to die. A low-intensity struggle on the couch followed. Peregrine's character died. "Fine," she said, relinquishing control. "Took me an hour to reach that spot. You have to start over."

"What about the save?"

"You're not burning my respawn count," grabbing for the controller. "Start your own."

This was sorted eventually. Heath began a game, Peregrine watching. There was another controller for two-player action somewhere. Peregrine couldn't be bothered to hunt for it.

"You're in better spirits," she finally said.

"Am I?" Heath said. His character very nearly died.

"You've been a lump of blackest coal for weeks, spitting barely suppressed hatred from the shotgun seat on all our deliveries, and no fun at parties."

"I haven't been going to any parties."

"Exactly," she said, drew a deep and very heartfelt breath. "You're allowed to tell me things, you know."

"I know."

"Make me worry. I'm not going to bite your head off—whatever it is—and I am definitely not going to narc."

Heath couldn't focus on the screen. He was fairly certain that his character died. "Sorry," he managed.

"My mum passing notes for you," said taking the controller back, switching to a racing game. "She's loving that, by the way," which was very true. Magpie was enjoying every minute of it.

"I don't think she understands how this whole discreet-note thing is supposed to work."

"And thank you for making me worry so much that I've resorted to digging information out of my mum."

"Sorry," Heath muttered. He tried to brush shoulders with her. Peregrine hit him with the controller. "How much has she told you?"

"That the notes are going to someone from another clan." She didn't look at him, eyes only for the screen. "That's not much of a surprise. Your mom's school . . . secret notes . . . takes all kinds."

"Clan Amaryllis," he whispered, as if saying the words would trigger an alarm hidden in the smoke detector. "Met him at the goat trials."

"We hate them, right? I can never keep track."

"Technically we hate them all, but yes, Amaryllis is on the do-not-resuscitate list."

"What are you doing, man?"

It was a fair question. He could be banished. He didn't want to answer. "Sorry," he managed.

"Didn't come to me."

"I did—I mean, I tried."

"What?" On the screen, her car crashed. It was a spectacular wreck.

"Over breakfast, I tried." He couldn't see. Peregrine was a blur, looking at him, all he could tell. "Remember questions about reed pipes?"

"Why would I remember questions about—"

"During the goat trials," interrupting. His fingers flailed at her, curled, practically a fist. "I tried—questions about music."

"Goat trials explains it," she said. "I wouldn't remember about music."

"No, never, you would never," flailing. She grabbed his wrists. "Never care about music."

"Okay," she said, and her arms were around him now. "I never noticed the music. You care about the music. I never noticed you trying." She could barely talk.

"Never cared about the music," he said, crying. "Nobody cares about the music."

"Nobody," she managed.

"Cares about the music."

"Stupid bloody music," holding him tight. They were both crying, silent sobs.

The car had respawned. It sat idle, the race ignored.

They disentangled themselves from the couch at

last, Peregrine switching the television off, and then she disappeared into the kitchenette, made coffee, found day-old muffins. She brought everything to the dining counter. It was more of a nook. They didn't really have a dining room or a proper table for eating.

Heath joined her at the dinner nook, perching on one of the stools. They nibbled muffins, sipped coffee. The only sounds were the sporadic sniffles and snorts that often followed after a good cry.

"This is no good," Peregrine eventually said, throwing down her muffin. "We should go out," meaning the communal cafeteria. "Get some proper food." That they didn't have to cook.

"In a bit," Heath replied, holding up his coffee mug, blowing over it.

Peregrine accepted this without comment, reached across the counter, gripped his hand. He tried to smile. They sipped their coffees.

It turned out to be late afternoon by the time they finally wandered away from their shared living environment, and the decision was very quickly made to go in search of the nearest bar. Those would serve food. It wouldn't be the best, relying heavily on grease and frying, but the place would serve alcohol. They found one not too far from the farming complex.

Technically, Clan Melaleuca frowned on the consumption of beer and other alcoholic beverages, mostly over the storage issue. Flammables were best kept away from the fire-breathing goats. Bars, wine bars, and other establishments happily took up residence as close to the farming complex as they dared. These tended to the cheekily named.

Peregrine and Heath went with Inflammable Storage. The burgers were decent. Sausages wrapped in bacon and grilled with peppers and onions were superior, and the beer was inexpensively palatable. Pool tables could be rented by the hour, and the coin-operated games were sufficiently vintage to be amusingly entertaining.

Ash November found them arguing over a table, Heath and Peregrine apparently having forgotten whether the current match was eight- or nine-ball. They sobered quickly under Ash's eye.

"I'll rack them up," Peregrine said, figuring abandonment of the current match was the best strategy. Heath nodded silent agreement and wandered in Ash's general direction.

"You weren't that hard to find," Ash said before Heath could manage the question.

"Creature of habit," Heath muttered. There was music, but it was more thumping bass than loud. Raised voices were not required.

"It's been quite the day," Ash said. "Busy. Exhausting. I was called away early. You may have heard."

"I may have," Heath said, acknowledging the unspoken apology. It was the closest to one he was going to get in public. "Relax." Heath indicated the table.

Peregrine almost said something, catching herself in time. They were expecting Queue and Mangrove Hatfield-Volker to join them at some point in the not-too-distant future.

"Have to go back," Ash said. "There was another incident."

"No."

Peregrine abandoned the table, came around to stand next to Heath. "How many is that?" she asked.

"Four—that we know of." Ash looked tired.

"Can't be—three," Heath said.

"Another clan's territory. We do occasionally share information."

"This is getting out of hand—"

"How does this keep happening?" Peregrine asked.

"I wish I knew." Ash had a hand to his face, scratching at his forehead. He looked very tired. "It's starting to affect the goats. They know something's up, getting harder to control."

"That's . . . not good," Heath said.

"I know."

"That's something of an understatement," Peregrine said.

"I know." Ash's hand was back in his hair. "That's why we're throwing more resources at this. Investigating. Asking questions. Digging deep. Having people followed."

"Oh," Heath said, feeling cold, wondering that his hands did not shake holding the pool cue. Peregrine tried not to give him a look, failing.

"You'll be questioned—expect to be questioned—I don't know when. About the first encounter—"

"Got it."

"—because you were there," Ash said.

"Figured that part."

"Thought you should know."

"Thank you."

"Wanted to tell you."

"I understand," Heath said, wanting to reach out, desperate to touch Ash, standing stock-still.

Ash said no more. He stood quiet for another moment, swaying ever so slightly with a hand to his head, rubbing the back of his neck. Then he turned, leaving them.

Peregrine started to say something, Heath shushing her without a sound. Peregrine followed his gaze, watching Ash, finding Cassandra Laughingstock near the entrance. She was watching them, waiting for Ash. They left together.

It was only after they were gone that Heath felt he could breathe again, releasing the breath that he had been holding, shoulders sagging. Peregrine turned to him as if she would speak, words failing.

"Lessons?" she finally managed, meaning Clan Amaryllis.

"No, that's not it," Heath said, feeling his eyes burn. "He was saying goodbye."

"No," reaching for him.

"Well, not *goodbye*-goodbye," taking her hand, holding it. "More like a break until things settle down."

"Reed masters and dung shovelers don't mix."

Heath didn't answer. There was no need for one. They abandoned the match, found a booth off in a corner, ordered more beer. Queue and Mangrove appeared eventually. Halfhearted attempts at revelry followed with mixed degrees of success.

Crisis

Heath made his way back to the fountain, the conjoined streets, and the scattered tables. Chardonnay was there, performing, as the notes exchanged via Magpie Volker had predicted. People had gathered, sitting at the tables, resting on the steps when there were no more tables. They listened. They sipped various beverages. The cafés loved it.

Heath waited. Chardonnay put away his reed pipes at last.

"You're early," Chardonnay said.

"I wanted to listen," looking about. "They wanted to listen."

"The crowd grows."

"I could join you," Heath said. "Duet."

"Later." The word was clipped short.

"I know." He knew he wasn't ready. "I didn't actually mean now."

"True," gathering his things. "You are making progress."

"Also true." Hearing Chardonnay say it out loud made it feel more real.

They went in search of the little two-seat spitfire. Chardonnay drove. Without the need for Arabesque to act as bodyguard and chaperon, there was more than enough room for two in the little car.

"This is getting risky," Heath said, trying to be heard over the sounds of the road and the car.

"I'm not as bad as Arabesque," Chardonnay replied, meaning his driving.

"No, the lessons, the meetings," Heath tried to explain. "They're tightening the screws, paranoia settling in."

"Has there been another?"

"No, I don't know. Nobody knows what's happening."

"The goats are acting out, harder to control."

"Everything out of control," Heath muttered, Chardonnay straining to hear. "I used to think—" turning, looking at Chardonnay. "Can you believe I used to think they really wanted me out of the reed-pipe chorus?"

"I don't—" Chardonnay tried to look at him, studying the road.

"How far would they go?" Heath said, words bursting from him.

"Surely," doubtful, appalled.

"So fast, they got there so fast—the goatherds—to catch the rogue goat," fumbling. "Like they knew. That first time. As if they had planned it."

"They wouldn't have let things carry on," Chardonnay said, dodging cars, having neglected to watch for cars. "Just to cover their tracks. Let things spiral out of control."

"I know," trying to breathe.

"Good," Chardonnay said, the car under control. "We are not at the center of this storm. It will pass."

"I don't know how long," thinking of Ash, missing him, stumbling over words. "We may have to curtail the lessons."

"If only there was somewhere we could meet," Chardonnay said. "Somewhere people were less concerned about students from various clans mingling."

"My mother," Heath tried to say.

"Affront to her ego, I know. My lessons are . . . rough, shall we say?" Chardonnay made a face as if remembering a wretched smell. "Trying to grind those crazy notions out of me."

"I don't know what happens if we're"—almost bit his tongue—"caught."

"Doubt they could take the fountain away from me," tried to say more, stumbled. "Doesn't help you, I know."

"Doesn't help me."

They reached the old streets. They found the back alley, parked the car, climbed the crooked stairs, found an awkward door. It only groaned a little.

The room never seemed to change. The table was forever strewn with papers. There was a box. That was new. Chardonnay went right to it, picked it up.

"This will help on the communication front." He tried to hand Heath the package. It was a mobile phone. Heath stepped back as if the package might burn him. "I've never understood your clan's aversion to phones," Chardonnay said.

"It's just not done." Heath took another involuntary step back.

"It's really weird," holding the phone out more firmly, daring Heath to take it. "We need to be able to communicate."

"Magpie will be crushed."

"Then we'll keep trading notes just to keep her happy." Chardonnay poked him with the box. "If things get rough, we need to be able to reach each other. I have . . . contingency plans."

"Contingency," Heath muttered.

"The falling out with Lady Rainchild, my own clan's concerns," said as if listing off unwelcome points. "I had to consider what would happen if things continued to go downhill," poking him again with the box. "I had to be ready."

"They're following me," Heath said as if the box was a torture device Chardonnay was threatening to use. Chardonnay did not move, frozen, as if he had forgotten how to breathe. "Oh, I don't know—I don't know. Maybe . . . I don't know."

"We need to be able to reach each other."

"If I'm found with it," reaching for the phone, fingers trembling.

"Hide it somewhere." Chardonnay tapped a note taped to the box. "That's my number." Heath stared blankly at it. "Oh, you don't know how to use it," taking the box back, sitting at the table, opening it.

"The school has a phone," Heath said, trying to sound helpful, failing.

"Landline, I know. This is a burner," holding up the phone. "We don't even have to talk. Probably better. Just DM each other." Chardonnay watched the blank look migrate toward fear. "Direct message, I'll show you. Very discreet. Very quiet."

The planned reed-pipe lesson mutated into an introductory mobile-phone tutorial. The reed-pipe lesson would have gone better.

Heath decided not to tell Cassandra Laughingstock about the burner phone. They were supposed to meet on a schedule. The easiest solution would have been to run into each other at Lady Rainchild's school, since they were both technically reed-pipe students, but it turned out she didn't spend much time there. Cassandra was too advanced. Her lessons required the involvement of actual fire-breathing goats of death, which was simply not going to happen anywhere near the school. Also, she didn't teach.

The meetings involved random back alleys and hallways around the clan farming complex, which seemed to suit Cassandra's whole approach to the situation. Peregrine had finally talked Heath into letting her tag along.

"What's with the girlfriend?" Cassandra said, stepping from shadows in a dark and seldom-used hallway in the rafters of a feed-storage barn.

"I don't trust you," Peregrine said.

"She doesn't trust you," Heath echoed. Peregrine had uttered more than a few harsh words upon discovering Heath and Cassandra held the clandestine meetings. "Also, she's not my girlfriend."

"Would you date your brother?" Peregrine was prepared to get right in Cassandra's face.

"Not even if I had one," Cassandra said. "Well, I do have one—more than one, I think—but I prefer not to contemplate their existence."

"See, things like that are why she doesn't trust you," Heath said.

"Why I don't trust you," Peregrine echoed.

"You just don't know me," Cassandra said to Peregrine. "After everything we've been through, you would think trust might be on offer," said to Heath.

"Cassie," he retorted. Cassandra winced.

"Yeah, okay, point taken," she said. "Please don't call me that."

"I haven't earned the right," he said by way of explanation to Peregrine, which wasn't actually necessary. Peregrine had gotten it through context and body language. "Trust is wobbling on the table."

"I love my siblings, by the way," Cassandra replied. "In that love/hate way that runs through all families. You two aren't technically related. Only child," pointing at Heath.

"True," said with a shrug.

"Siblings in all but blood," Peregrine said. "Less of that love/hate thing you've got going on with your dysfunctional family and more mutual love and respect over here."

"Meaning you'd die for him?" Cassandra asked. "Move mountains, cross oceans, and all of that?"

"That's a question?" Peregrine replied.

"Guess not," Cassandra said, pointing at Heath. "Lessons, how are they going?"

"Harder to schedule because of the scrutiny and paranoia," Heath said. "Otherwise going well."

"Let me hear it."

Heath produced his reed pipes, unwrapping them, brought them to his lips.

"Scales," Cassandra said, catching him mid-breath. He sighed, took a fresh breath, started a scale. Sound-dampening qualities were why they held the meetings in such unusual locations. "Highland's Fourth Étude," interrupting a scale.

Heath had to think, pulling at his memory. "Chardonnay doesn't like Highland," he said.

"What a shock," Cassandra replied. "Lady Rainchild would have assigned it. Unless it's above your level."

"Rude," Peregrine said.

"No, it's a fair point," Heath said with a sigh and then began to play.

"Rusty," Cassandra said. "Loosen your fingering. You're tight."

"You should be a teacher," Peregrine said. Heath almost dropped a note.

"I hate students," Cassandra replied.

"And they would love you."

"Now the Sixth Étude," Cassandra said, leaning against the wall with a hand over her eyes. Heath tried to remember and play. There were lots of runs, skips, and arpeggios. "Lady Rainchild loves that one."

"Was that an insult?" Peregrine said. "Sounded like an insult."

"It needs work," Heath said, apologetic.

"He's self-aware," Cassandra said. "Now," rubbing at her temples, "let's hear one of Chardonnay's creations. He's been teaching you those, yes?"

"I don't know—"

"Someone needs to know what that outsider is putting in your head," interrupting him. "And you're not playing them for Lady Rainchild. I know that without guessing."

Heath took a slow breath, shaking, giving him a moment to collect his thoughts. He tried to think of the numbers that Chardonnay had played for him, something soft, something thoughtful, and he began to play. He felt the swelling in his chest like a lost soul, letting the melody drift, feeling notes more than remembering them. Closing his eyes, he couldn't look at them. When he brought the song to a close and risked a look, he saw that the hand had drifted, falling, from Cassandra's eyes.

"That," she started to say, words drifting, and then caught herself. "Thank you."

"That was beautiful," Peregrine said.

"He doesn't seem to have caused too much damage," Cassandra said. "That's good, but I'm still concerned about these meetings. The investigators are becoming aggressive."

"We're well aware of that," Heath said, trying to hold his voice steady. He had started finding faces in shadows, even though there were none. "I can retreat to my mother's home if things get bad. It's neutral territory."

"That's . . . drastic," sounding doubtful. "What about the meetings? They're still in Amaryllis territory."

"We're prepared to let time slide, depending on how agitated the investigators become."

"Why can't they get to the bottom of the rogue goat

issue?" Peregrine asked, downright angry. "It's smug-glers, right? Some kind of clandestine agent?"

"I don't . . . know," Cassandra said, looking pained. "They're not sharing their investigative strategies with me, and Ash isn't letting anything drop. He's very stressed, that's all I know."

They all knew one of the techniques Cassandra was using to help with Ash's stress, but Heath didn't want to think about it, and Peregrine managed to resist commenting. She knew how much the separation was bothering him.

"It'll blow over," Peregrine said when they were some distance from the storage building and well away from Cassandra. "Investigative fires burn hot and bright and quickly burn down to embers."

Heath didn't want to answer.

"Not if the goats keep fanning the flames," he coun-tered, unable to help himself. "It's so weird."

"I know," Peregrine said, putting her arm around him, holding, squeezing. There was nothing more to say.

Heath didn't see Ash until weeks later, coming home after a long shift delivering flaming pellets. It had been some time. Ash was standing inside the com-munal space Heath shared with Peregrine. The typical plan after a hard day was to clean up, change, and go in search of food or entertainment. They were scheduled to meet up with Queue and Mangrove Hatfield-Volker and go in search of an evening's diversion.

Ash looked as if he had been pacing, unable to hold still, waiting. Heath was surprised. Ash didn't normally let himself into the shared space. Peregrine half-stum-bled into the room behind Heath, unclear on the ob-struction.

Ash held up the burner phone before Heath could get a word out. Heath felt the floor give. Peregrine recognized that Ash held a phone and kept her thoughts to herself.

"What's the code?" Ash said.

"It's not—"

"Someone's been trying to reach you," interrupting, looking at the screen.

"—mine."

"Whoever set this up for you was smart enough to only let it display that there are messages waiting," Ash continued. "No previews."

"I found it," Heath said. "I thought maybe it could play games or something if I could figure out how to open it."

Peregrine was shying sideways like she wanted to stand next to him and face Ash, but Heath was on fire, and she didn't want to get burned.

"I figure it's Chardonnay Chalice," Ash said, still studying the screen. "Trying to warn you."

"Who's Chardonnay—"

"We've had you under surveillance," interrupting again, angry. Heath could only study the floor. "First flaming-pellet team to encounter the rogue goat, of course we had you watched. When confronted with the facts—pictures—Cassandra Laughingstock gave you up. I'm trying to decide if she knew about the phone."

"She didn't," Heath said, almost shouting. "Peregrine either."

"Don't tell me what I did and did not know," Peregrine countered.

He spun on her. "You didn't know."

"Maybe Ash's not the only one to search your room."

"Don't say that," whispering.

"But I didn't find it in your room, Peregrine Volker," Ash said. "I found it in his. Hardly hidden at all. You would have moved it."

Peregrine didn't answer.

"Investigators can't connect you to the baby-goat ring," Ash said to Heath. "But this," meaning the phone. "Consorting with Clan Amaryllis." He couldn't continue.

Heath tried desperately to remember the last time he had met Chardonnay at the fountain. It was before the phone, he was almost sure. There had been faces in the shadows. The investigators might not know about the fountain. There had been faces in the crowd. Nobody was speaking.

"Not Clan Amaryllis," Heath said to fill the silence. They looked at him. "Just Chardonnay Chalice."

"Same difference."

"They don't like his music either."

"I know all about his *music*," last word said with a sneer. "It's why they were grateful for the tip. Clan Amaryllis has been looking for a reason to move on him."

"No," Heath tried to say, the word slipping away from him like a forgotten thing.

"Council's waiting," Ash said, meaning the clan leadership board.

"Can I?" Heath looked at himself, hoping for a chance to clean up, look presentable before leadership while they passed judgment on him.

"No," Ash answered. Heath's heart fell through the floor. "You're staying here," Ash said, turning on Peregrine.

"Family," Peregrine said, moving, standing next to Heath.

"You're not," Ash countered.

"Stay," Heath tried to say, and realized Peregrine was grinding her fists. She was going to punch Ash in the face. "Think of your mom."

"Don't tell me what to do," she shouted, but moved away as if he had struck her.

"Let's go," he said to Ash, and they left the shared

suite. They could hear the coffee table being smashed. The flatmates wouldn't like that.

They walked. Ash could have brought a car, but they walked. There could have been others waiting to escort them, but it was just the two of them.

"She had nothing to do with this," Heath said, meaning Peregrine, when he couldn't stay quiet any longer. "She doesn't know anything."

"We'll see," Ash replied, clipped, short, like he was trying to stay calm.

"She wasn't going to hit you."

"No, no, she was, I could tell."

"She doesn't like you. Doesn't like any of the reed masters, really."

"I gathered that."

"I'm cooperating, see?" Heath said, wanting to turn, knowing better than to look at Ash. They had been a semi-secret couple for years. "You don't have to threaten Peregrine or her mom to get me to talk."

"We'll see."

"Anything—"

"What's the code for the phone?" Ash asked, interrupting. Heath didn't answer. "That's what I thought."

There was a central office building, almost like a center of government for the clan. It was big and imposing, stone and marble, painted white and gold. The water towers flanking it were more ornamental than functional, looking like ceremonial guards. Heath and Ash walked past it, the building, the towers.

"I used to think—" Heath said. He couldn't help himself, watching the administration building fade away. "The first rogue goat was a setup. Excuse to take the reed-pipe chorus away from me." Ash made a noise that was half dismissive snort and half bitter laugh. "The goatherds—control team—got there so fast."

"There was no setup," Ash said.

"I know," Heath whispered, hollow, his voice in pain. "But I can't stop thinking," wishing his voice would give out. "Can't let it go."

There was another building, an administrative annex past the central office building, an extension of the massive goat pens. Heath couldn't take his eyes off it, the annex. The clan fed dissidents and outcasts to the goats. They were walking toward it.

"How did they get there so fast?" Heath said.

"What?" Ash stopped dead in his tracks, rounding on him.

"They were ready," unable to stop the flow of words. "In all their gear. Like they knew."

Ash hit him. Heath found himself on the cold, hard ground, tasting blood in his mouth. He spat it out, otherwise he didn't move.

"Get up," Ash said, more growl than command.

Heath looked up. The annex and goat pens were before them. Flames sparked the evening, radiating into the sky. It was never dark. It was never quiet.

Crawling to his feet, he stood. Ash did nothing to help him. They walked, Heath unsteadily, to the annex and to the flames that burned the sky.

The hallways were narrow and dark, and they smelled. The few people they saw were bruisers. They looked like poorly disguised guards ready to beat Heath half to death at a moment's notice. Heath found his feet dragging. He tripped once or twice, even fell into the wall at one point as if he couldn't walk straight. His mouth hurt. He tasted nothing but blood.

They stopped before one door. It was unremarkable. It was unadorned.

"Passcode," Ash said. "Last chance."

"I won't hurt anyone," Heath said, trembling, shaking, feeling blood slip down his chin. "Anything I've done, I'll say if it's true, but I won't name names. Let you hurt them."

"That's not what happens here," Ash said harshly, almost hissing the words as if trying desperately to control himself. He couldn't look at Heath. He almost couldn't talk. He hit the door with his fist as if he had forgotten how to knock.

The door opened. There was a table. There was a depression in the floor as if someone had started to dig, forgetting they stood on wood. Masons had worked to repair the floor and leave something of a lowered pit. Heath was made to stand there, facing the table.

There was Marshall November, looking severe, looking angry. There was Vladimir Cyclone, looking angry, looking jubilant. There was Clementine Fortinbras-Cyclone, looking bored, looking severe, and there was Hannibal Greenswallow, looking tired, looking determined.

"Such a waste," Vladimir Cyclone said. Heath's uncle was dependably condescending and crude.

Heath spat blood on the floor. "I've done nothing wrong," he said.

"That's naive to the point of idiocy," Ash said, almost shouting, as if he would soon lose the war with anger. He joined the others at the table, throwing the phone onto its surface for all to see, taking a seat next to Clementine Fortinbras-Cyclone.

"Reed-pipe students are supposed to interact," Heath said, holding his chin up, daring them to notice the blood. "It's the whole point of the school."

"Calls himself a student," Vladimir said.

"You weren't at the school," Marshall November said.

"Lady Rainchild is my teacher," Heath said. "I am at the school. I am a student."

"Should we make you play for us?" Marshall November asked. "Demonstrate that you are a student of the great Lady Rainchild Cyclone-Claymore?"

"If that's what it takes." He realized he was still carrying the satchel with his father's reeds. Everything happening so fast, there had been no time to put them down. He couldn't play for them like he had for Cassandra weeks before. His mouth hurt.

"Is he holding reed pipes right now?" Hannibal Greenswallow said as if Heath wasn't in the room. "Take them," indicating big men—bruisers—by the wall.

They took the satchel. They weren't gentle. The satchel was dropped on the table next to the phone. Nobody touched either.

"Prove you've taken lessons?" Vladimir Cyclone said. "Perhaps," sneering. "Prove they were lessons with Lady Rainchild and not Chardonnay Chalice?" Heath couldn't look at them. "No."

"You are banished, simple as that," Ash November said. "Nothing but the clothes on your back. Money, identification . . . belong to the clan."

The bruisers roughed him up, searching his pockets, taking his things, taking everything. He couldn't resist, fight back. He wanted to look at Ash, shout questions about the other rogue goats, ask how long it had taken the goatherd teams to arrive. His jaw hurt. He couldn't look at Ash. He couldn't say anything. They tied his hands as a last step.

"If you are found in Clan Melaleuca territory," Ash November said, "you will be dealt with," meaning they would feed him to the goats.

Heath nodded his head. He couldn't hold his eyes open. He couldn't even spit.

"Lady Rainchild's home, the school," his uncle Vladimir Cyclone said, "is Clan Melaleuca territory."

The gasp—sharp, strong, loud—escaped him before he could stop it. He could not look at them.

He was led from the room, a rope tied to his wrists. The bruisers were not gentle. He was all but dragged off his feet. He stumbled down hallways. The lighting was bad. He crashed into walls. He almost fell. He found himself outside.

There was a car. They placed him in the back seat, and they drove. They didn't stop for a long time. He wasn't even sure where he was when they let him out. They didn't bother to unbind his hands. They drove away.

Heath slumped, stumbling, falling, and found himself sitting on the curb. Trembling took him. He couldn't hold still, couldn't stop shaking. He wanted to cry out, scream, but he couldn't. His mouth refused to work. He couldn't voice words. He still tasted blood. His head fell to his hands. He could feel the rope against his forehead.

It felt very late when he could look up at last. It was a dirt street. It smelled. Light was bad. Buildings loomed. There were people. There weren't many, but they were there, walking, keeping to themselves, avoiding him.

Heath stood, started walking. He had an idea where he was. He could find his mother's home. It would take a long time. It wasn't Clan Melaleuca territory. Heath didn't care what his uncle claimed. It was a sanctuary.

It was so late that it might as well have been morning when Heath finally reached his mother's home. There were many doors. He went for one as far from the school side as possible. It was practically a servant's door.

"That's far enough," someone said. The way was guarded. Heath didn't recognize who it was.

"I'm looking for Magpie Volker," Heath said.

"She went home, hours ago," the stranger said, towering over him.

"This is her home." Heath couldn't stop trembling. He didn't know how long he could stand.

"Family emergency, something about her daughter."

"No," barely a whisper. Heath tried to stand tall, hands still bound. "This is my home."

"Maybe once," the stranger said. "Consorting with rival clans. Maybe one of them will take you."

"This is my home," whispering, feeling broken and bent.

"This doesn't have to be a warning." The stranger sounded like he meant it.

Heath wanted to cry. He couldn't cry. He couldn't stop shaking. He didn't understand why he wasn't a collapsed heap, sobbing, a broken thing. He didn't ask for his mother. He turned. He wandered away, a direction without a destination.

The stars were fading, the sky turning red as if slowly soaking with blood when he stopped. He could barely stand. He could not walk anymore. Heath looked about, swaying, realizing he did not recognize anything or know where he stood. The streets were alien. The buildings had the look of uncaring offices towering over him.

He forced himself to move just a little more, finding a narrow way between office buildings. There were trash dumpsters in a corner, flats of ripped and discarded cardboard stacked nearby. He tried to drag several sheets of the cardboard even farther back into the corner. Everything smelled.

He had seen lost souls do this before, out of the corner of his eye while walking the streets or doing the flaming-pellet rounds with Peregrine. People huddled under cardboard, trying to wrap it around themselves.

He couldn't stand. The cardboard was not comfortable. He did not care. Maybe a piece of the thin board stayed folded over him. He did not know. He had to rest.

He knew he should not close his eyes. It was very nearly morning. There would be people. There would be danger. He had to rest.

Heath dreamed of the dancing men.

They were elegant and fluid, moving like dandelion seeds carried by the wind. Their clothes billowed and flowed around them. Ribbons and streamers swirled. Jewels sparkled on their skin like miniature stars that had been plucked from the sky.

In his dream, the dancing men took the cardboard. They wrapped him in cloaks and robes. They draped blankets around him.

They fed him soup and gave him nectar to drink.

"Why?" Heath said in his dream.

"Our gift to you," they answered, as only dreams can answer. "We would never abandon you."

"I don't deserve," he tried to say. "I am nothing."

"Nothing is only a word," they retorted, amused. They never stopped moving. They were the billowing tide.

"Thank you," he whispered in dream.

"Our gift to you," they said, holding reed pipes out to him. They rippled like sunlight through wind-touched branches and leaves.

"No, I cannot," trying to push them away. His fingers brushed through the hands holding the reed pipes as if pushing through a lace curtain. "I am worthless."

"Worth is only a word," they chided, teasing.

"The goats do not listen," he said, feeling the reed pipes in his hands. "I cannot control them."

"They like you anyway."

He cried in the way one does in dreams, sobbing without tears. "Thank you," Heath said.

"Go to the fountain," they said, moving back. They were already so far away.

"What fountain?" Heath called out to them as if he stood on a pinnacle overlooking grand canyons, hearing the echoes of his own voice drift back to him.

"You know which one," nothing more than whispers on the distant wind, and then they were gone, in the way of all dreams.

Revelations

When Heath woke, he found he was still in the back alley, office buildings towering over him, wrapped in the blankets the dancing men had left him, wearing the robes they had given him.

There was a knapsack. He found it packed with food, bread, cheese, dried fruit, chocolate, and seasoned meat. There was a thermos of nectar and another of tea. There was a purse filled with money. Some of the coins looked very old. Some of the bills looked brand new.

The reed pipes were wrapped in scarves. He had never seen their like.

Everything fit into the knapsack. Even the blankets seemed to fold into themselves until they were a bundle no more round than his fist.

Heath looked around, standing at the edge of the narrow way, looking at the road, trying to figure where he was, and he finally realized that the ropes no longer bound his hands. Heath wandered until he found a public transit stop. It didn't take long.

The bus driver was kind enough to explain he had somehow managed to wander deep into the financial district and advised him on the number of transfers needed to reach the fountain. The trip took some time. Heath dozed on the bus, feeling he was still half lost to dreams.

He reached the neighborhood of the fountain at last. The streets were the familiar brick and stone. The buildings were rugged and old, casting quiet shadows, breathing ancient breaths of soft, cool air. There was the siren call of familiar reed-pipe music.

Chardonnay Chalice sat on the steps of the fountain as if nothing had changed. His eyes were closed. The song was haunting and achingly beautiful. The people gathered at the café tables listened, drinks ignored.

The melody drifting to a close, Chardonnay opened his eyes and saw Heath watching him from the far edge of the tables. Chardonnay jumped to his feet. The song forgotten, shattered, notes fluttering as if suddenly cut adrift and lost to the evening air. Chardonnay ran to him, threw his arms around him, hugging him tight, saying nothing. Heath could not answer, could not even raise his arms to embrace Chardonnay. The audience began to mutter at their tables, wondering what had just happened, wishing for more music.

"I couldn't reach you," Chardonnay managed. "They cut off my phone service," meaning Clan Amaryllis. "Even the backup."

"They took my phone," Heath said, meaning it did not matter.

"I couldn't get close to Lady Rainchild, the school."

"Neither could I."

"What happened to you?" Chardonnay held him at arm's length, looking him over. "Where did you go?"

"I wandered."

"You look tired."

"It's been a long night."

"It's been days," Chardonnay said, beginning to maneuver toward one of the tables. The audience made room for them, moving so that Heath and Chardonnay would have the illusion of privacy. "Days and days."

"It was only yesterday," Heath said, starting to wonder.

"How long were you wandering?" Chardonnay tried

to laugh, looking very concerned. "What happened? Look at you," meaning everything Heath was wearing.

"Gifts of the dancing men." Heath tried to make it sound unimportant, realizing how outlandish he must look. The bus driver had been very kind not to have made a scene.

"The dancing men?" Chardonnay said around a sharp intake of breath, sounding bewildered and amazed.

"I thought it was a dream," Heath said, raising his arms like a shrug, looking at the sleeves of his robes. "Some dream."

"They helped you? Spoke to you?" Surprise and bewilderment giving way to awe.

"And all I had to do was wander the streets until I was half mad."

"Their ways are mysterious, and their reasons not to be understood," Chardonnay said. "But they are kind."

"Mysterious is putting it mildly," Heath answered. "Kind? For all we know, they created the fire-breathing goats of death and set them loose upon the world just to see what would happen."

"They helped you," Chardonnay said. "All that matters."

"Banished," Heath said, raising his arms. The sleeves of his robes slipped from his arms, and he realized that the markings and tattoos that had covered his body for as long as he could remember were gone. He grabbed at his arms, hands slipping, sliding over skin, fingers searching for the scars. He made a sound like a haunted creature that could easily blossom into a wail.

"Wondrous strange," Chardonnay said, grabbing him, pushing the robe way up Heath's arm as if the tattoos were hiding near his shoulder.

"I don't . . . understand," Heath managed.

"Let's get you away from here." Chardonnay stood.

"Somewhere you can rest. The cafés will wonder why I've stopped playing." Heath stood. They started walking, Chardonnay guiding. "They pay me—the café owners—as long as I draw crowds to sit and eat and drink and listen."

"Contingency plans?" Heath asked, staggering, walking.

"Yes, until Clan Amaryllis figures out how to lean on the café owners. Shut me down." They entered one of the cafés, moving quickly through the dining area, reaching the back. "I don't know if they've found this place yet. They may not care."

They moved through the kitchen, found winding narrow stairs in the back. They climbed, reached a landing, a row of doors, and settled upon one door. It held a small room, barely large enough for a narrow bed, tiny table, and cramped chair. Chardonnay maneuvered Heath onto the bed. The knapsack was placed on the chair.

"I have to go back," Chardonnay said, sounding like he wanted to do nothing of the sort. "Play for my supper, so to speak, and then I help with the washing up. It doesn't pay well."

Chardonnay left, closing the door. Heath drifted. He may have slept. Everything was a muddled fog of a wakeful dream. The dancing men didn't bother him.

Chardonnay returned at some point. Heath wasn't sure. Chardonnay barely had strength to crawl onto the bed, Heath making room for him somehow. It may have been part of the dream.

Heath woke to the smell of coffee. Chardonnay was perched on the cramped chair. There were two cups on the small table. There was coffee. There were bacon sandwiches. The coffee was hot. Heath went for the sandwich. He felt like he hadn't eaten in forever.

"There's a thermos with tea, I think," Heath said.

Chardonnay looked puzzled. "In the bag. It holds more than it looks."

Chardonnay started to sort through the bag. "A lot more than it looks," he managed. "We'll be days sorting this."

"I hope we have days," said around bits of sandwich. He had started to work on half of Chardonnay's own.

"We have days."

"What will you do?"

"Continue to play for my supper," Chardonnay said while slowly pulling things from the knapsack. "I enjoy it. Gain notice. I was growing a following even before the clan disowned me."

"So, what you had been doing, but harder?" There were no more bacon sandwiches.

"What I had been doing, but harder," Chardonnay said. "I have stashes of money. At least I hope I still have stashes," mumbling. "They may have found them. They keep finding my phones."

"There's a purse in there somewhere," meaning the knapsack. "They can't take that."

"They can try." Chardonnay pointed to the purse resting half-open on a corner of the bed. "We should resist spending the dancing men's gift funds for as long as possible. There could be unanticipated consequences."

"True." Heath hadn't thought of that and frantically tried to remember how many coins he had used for bus fare.

"What will you do?" Chardonnay continued sorting and examining so that Heath could think without being stared at.

"I don't . . . I don't," Heath said. "I've barely had any time."

"Only a day or so for you, I know," Chardonnay said. "You should ease into things."

"I don't . . . burden."

"You're not a burden," countered quietly.

"I could help downstairs," Heath said. "If they'll have me. Free you from the washing up. Time to rest."

"Give me time to rest," said wistfully.

"Time for lessons." Heath took the knapsack, found the reed pipes. "They gave me these," holding the bundle of scarves out to Chardonnay.

"They gave you these?" Chardonnay said, drawing breath slow, reaching for the reed pipes with tentative fingers as if proximity would cause them to tarnish and melt.

"They're not my father's reeds, but they will do."

"I will," touching the reed pipes with nothing more than his fingertips. "I will speak with the café owners about work."

They rested, sipping coffee, admiring the reed pipes. Chardonnay showed Heath where the communal washroom and shower were located. Chardonnay went out while Heath rested, returning with more suitable clothes. Heath was able to move into one of the adjoining rooms. Chardonnay went back downstairs to help in the kitchen. Heath rested.

He clambered down at last, wanting to be helpful. They put him to work. Chardonnay went to prepare for his afternoon performance. Chardonnay would sit before the fountain, entertain and serenade the café patrons sipping their coffees, eating their food, listening to the music.

The lessons began days later, when they could fit time into their café and kitchen duties. Heath progressed quickly. The new reed pipes were a dream to work with. The café staff started encouraging Heath and Chardonnay to perform together. The crowds grew.

Chardonnay's cousin, Arabesque, was the first to

reach out to them, found them performing before the fountain. Arabesque simply joined the audience gathered around the tables, sipping drinks, listening. He took a note to Lady Rainchild's school. Messages were passed to Peregrine. She appeared at one of the tables with Arabesque one day. She didn't want to interrupt the concert.

The moment they finished, Peregrine was upon them, squeezing Heath even as he tried to stand. She was crying. Heath was crying. There were no words. It was some time before they could maneuver to a table, dislodging concert stragglers.

"You vanished," Peregrine managed, wiping at her face with a sleeve. "Nobody knows what happened."

Heath tried to explain, revealed his bare arms. Peregrine screamed. People jumped at their tables, scattering dishes. Calm was eventually restored.

"I doubt I'll ever be used to it," Heath said. "What about you? Did Ash protect you?"

"I quit," she said, as if daring him to challenge her. "Moved back with my mother. She needed me. Aunty Rainchild was an angry, enraged, furious mess. She threatened to ban all the Clan Melaleuca students."

"Good for her," Heath whispered.

"She yelled at her brother, *Lord Cyclone*," mocking. "I didn't know that was possible. It hurt her. I could tell. Because of the—" Peregrine indicated her forearms where Rainchild's scars and tattoos were hidden.

"Yes, I know."

"I don't want to go back," Peregrine said, looking about. "What do you do when you are not performing?"

"We help in the kitchens," he said with a shrug.

"I could do that."

"Your mother needs you," meaning his mother needed the support.

"I don't want to be . . . trapped," she whispered. "Family and clan will drown you whether they mean to or no."

"It doesn't have to be sudden. We shall wean them off you," Heath said. She looked uncomfortable. "If it starts to look like they won't let you go, we'll rip them off like a bandage."

Peregrine stayed into the evening. She even helped in the kitchen. The staff loved her. She left with Arabesque at last, vowing to return.

Peregrine did return, not very often at first, every few days. She would appear at one of the tables or helping in the kitchens or even serving the coffee and food. She was good with the patrons, remembering names and orders with ease.

Cassandra Laughingstock was the next to appear, Peregrine having passed begrudging word to her. Magpie Volker loved being in the middle of the clandestine movement of messages. Cassandra listened, sitting at one of the tables, sipping coffee.

"There's news," Cassandra told Heath and Chardonnay while they rested between sets. "Ash November has a lead on the goat smugglers. He's working with the special investigators behind the other counselor's backs."

"That's interesting." Heath tried to sound unconcerned. His jaw ached, for some reason, like a faint and faded memory.

"It's tricky business. I can't say more. Things could turn very badly for Ash if he's not careful."

Cassandra left. They had more sets to perform.

"Ash did throw you to the wolves," Peregrine said when Heath and Chardonnay told her the news. She had her own room—above one of the other cafés, best they could do—but still went back to her mother and the school more often than not.

"He did what he could," Heath countered, voice soft like he didn't mean it, defending out of old and rusty habit.

"You just don't want to hear it," Peregrine countered back, picking up on Heath's half-spoken tone, as if she might say more, as if she might know more, but not wanting to press too hard.

Chardonnay kept his thoughts to himself.

The café staff discovered that Peregrine used to play guitar—never very well or with any great skill—but they didn't care. A guitar appeared one day. Nobody would reveal who was responsible or how they had acquired it. The staff encouraged her to perform and got her to pluck away at it a little while they worked in the kitchen.

"I thought you said she wasn't musically inclined," Chardonnay said to Heath one day after discovering that Peregrine could sing.

"I said she had no ear for the reed pipes," he retorted.

"Maybe it's the clan's over-emphasis on music to control the goats."

Heath didn't answer. He could only shrug his shoulders in indifferent despair for everything the clans had ever done.

Ash November appeared one day, standing way back, listening. He didn't approach the tables. Cassandra had brought him. She approached the fountain, waited for a good moment between numbers, and made Heath aware of Ash's presence. Heath ignored him, hoping Ash might disappear as quietly as he had arrived, but he stayed. Ash stayed. He listened, and he stayed.

Heath accepted that Ash would not leave, almost missing a note when the realization struck. He finally wandered over during a break. Cassandra did not follow. Peregrine had taken to strumming the guitar between reed-pipe sets, strolling between the tables. The audience seemed to appreciate it. Cassandra did too.

Heath stopped, not wanting to get too close. Ash had bodyguards. Heath couldn't help but notice them standing there, trying to be inconspicuous. Chardonnay was somewhere, trying not to watch.

"Hey," Ash said, trying, failing to sound nonchalant.

"Hey yourself," Heath said, trying to sound uninterested and unimpressed, remembering a walk, remembering the taste of blood.

"You look—you sound . . . good," Ash said.

"We manage," said like it didn't matter.

"A lot has happened," said as if struggling for words.

"I wouldn't know," which was true. Cassandra had not shared updates on the investigation, if she had known anything. Peregrine learned nothing from her mother or the school on her rare visits back.

"We know what happened—we caught them." Ash looked uncomfortable. "It was Vladimir Cyclone—your uncle—my uncle, too, for that matter." He looked even more uncomfortable.

"Surprising," Heath said, meaning it was anything but a surprise. Ash looked as if he might throw up. Heath felt a deep root tug at his soul, wanting to reach out, wanting to comfort Ash, steady him with a touch, but he resisted, remembering blood. The root twisted and turned, but he stood firm.

"You were right," Ash said as if the words hurt him. "Got me thinking—why did you get me thinking? That first time—so fast—they got there so fast . . . like you said . . . like they knew," trailing away, bewildered.

"I hate being right," not really meaning it.

"They were experimenting," Ash said, swaying. "Some crazy plan to use young goat blood as an alternative power source. They were bleeding them," said, looking horrified. "Why the containment sheds kept exploding."

"That's . . . insane," Heath managed.

"So insane . . . They're awaiting sentencing. I'll probably have them fed to the goats."

"You?"

"Yes, didn't Cassie tell you? I'm clan leader now."

"No." Heath couldn't breathe, heart catching on every other beat like it would break. "She didn't."

"Matters not," Ash said, dismissive, standing tall. "The council folded—what's left of it—they folded. Do whatever I tell them." Ash took a deep breath as if gathering courage, making Heath worry. "You should come back," he said.

"No," Heath retorted, snapping out the word without thinking, stepping back. "I can't. I just can't."

"You can," Ash said, stepping forward. "You are Clan Melaleuca."

"No, not anymore."

"All is forgiven," spreading his arms, inviting.

"Matters not," Heath said, muttering, taking another step away. "I can't go back. I'm not Clan Melaleuca." He pulled at his sleeves, trying to work out how to undo buttons. "Not anymore," and then his forearms were free, enough to show the marks and scars were gone.

Ash drew breath as if he would choke on air, reaching out. Heath stepped back as Ash stepped forward. Ash froze, catching himself, and stood unmoving, looking without seeing. Heath said nothing. Ash lowered his arms, closed his eyes.

"What are you then?" said all but whispering. "Clan Amaryllis?"

"No," Heath said, also whispering. He remembered something discussed with Chardonnay late into the night. They had both been stretched upon the bed, propped on uncomfortable pillows. "Clan Calatheas."

"What?" Ash opened his eyes, snapped them open, and then studied the ground at Heath's feet.

"Call us Clan Calatheas," sounding more certain.

"A new clan—the future," Ash said. "This would be you and Chardonnay Chalice, more duet than clan."

"Peregrine makes three," Heath countered, feeling defiant, hearing his uncle in Ash's voice, remembering every sneered word and condescending glare from clan and family.

"That will be news to her mother," Ash said, meaning Heath's mother.

"She will be proud," Heath said, also meaning his mother. "Or she won't."

"I see," Ash said, looking up, taking a slow but deep-felt breath, matching Heath's eye. "Clan Melaleuca seeks no quarrel with Clan Calatheas."

"Clan Calatheas has no quarrel with you."

"Such are bonds of good relations between dissimilar clans formed," Ash said, formally, as if making a proclamation. Heath did not answer, did not comment that the proclamation didn't quite make sense. They were both emotional, trying to hide it, trying to put a good face on things. Ash turned—understanding there would be no formal answer—and left, his bodyguards following after.

Heath returned to the fountain, Chardonnay joining him. They had a set to complete, which they did.

Epilogue

Heath and Chardonnay booked a gig together—an actual gig, a late-evening post-work and post-supper actual paying gig. It was indoors and everything, a basement coffee house. The people came specifically to hear them. They weren't just playing before a fountain, whether the crowds wished it or no. The people still sat at tables—it was a coffeehouse, after all. They sipped coffee. They drank cocktails.

Heath and Chardonnay shared the stage, looking over the enraptured audience, playing reed pipes. Peregrine played guitar. They were a trio now. She even sang when the number called for it.

Rainchild Cyclone-Claymore had commandeered tables at the far end of the coffee house facing the stage. She said it was best for the acoustics, music traveling over the heads of most of the audience. There were booths, but Rainchild said the sound quality was bad. She preferred the tables.

She had brought some of the most promising students with her, representing a broad cross-section of the clans. She had also brought many of the teachers. Others came unbidden and had to fight for space at tables scattered across the coffee-house floor.

Cassandra Laughingstock was there with some of the more snobbish and high-ranking reed-pipe students. They were hard to miss, sitting at a table as close to the stage as they could get. There had been a more-than-a-little-heated debate over the best acoustics, but proximity to the performers had won out.

The performance was a hit. There had been clapping and cheering and calls for encores. Rainchild had screamed, waving her arms over her head. Heath found it hard to miss that her mother's outfit lacked sleeves. The scars, designs, and tattoos ran from her fingers to her shoulders. She didn't seem to mind that everybody could see.

Heath, Chardonnay, and Peregrine descended the stage. They were mobbed, people reaching, touching, hugging. There was a space that was not quite a backstage area for the performers. It gave them not-quite privacy. It also held Ash November.

Heath and Peregrine were laughing, intoxicated by the performance, but they stopped, growing still, when they realized who was there.

"We'll find Aunty Rainchild," Peregrine said, tapping Chardonnay on the shoulder. "We lost my mom out there somewhere. Aunty should know what happened to her."

Chardonnay took the hint.

"Clan Calatheas," Ash said after Peregrine and Chardonnay had departed.

"Clan Melaleuca," Heath answered. They almost had privacy.

"It was a good performance," Ash said, hesitantly, awkwardly. "Even Lady Rainchild seemed to enjoy it."

"I know."

"Your mother seems . . . happier. Like a burden has been lifted."

"You did feed her brother to the goats. She never liked him."

"It has made her strong, defiant—"

"She was always strong," interrupting. "She made the school what it is, taking students from every clan.

Nobody wanted that. Everyone fighting her, and yet she did it. Nobody gave her that."

"She's also a great reed-pipe master." Ash seemed to be marshaling thoughts, building up to a proposal. "You should come—"

"We've been over this," interrupting again. "No."

"I was going to say," as if fumbling for words, "that the goat trials are coming up."

"Has it been that long?" Heath said, surprised, feeling bewildered.

"It has," Ash replied, sounding as if he had found better footing. "Clan Calatheas should perform. As the head of Clan Melaleuca, I'm sure I could make that happen."

"That's . . . something," Heath said, feeling he should find a chair or a wall to lean against so that he did not fall. "I will have to discuss with Chardonnay and Peregrine."

"Of course."

"The exposure would be good for us. Lead to more gigs."

"Spend less time washing dishes," Ash said, hearing the words only after speaking them, looking about as if desperate to draw them back. "Are you expected to do the washing here?"

"No," Heath replied, "and you can drop the pretensions. Washing dishes and helping in kitchens is no worse than shoveling goat dung."

"I suppose that's true," Ash said. He appeared to be mustering his thoughts as if building to another pronouncement. "I miss you," he managed.

"I noticed," Heath said, looking out toward the audience, remembering a cold, dark night and cardboard boxes for a bed. "Everybody misses me," wistfully sarcastic.

"There must be something," floundering for words.

"I'm not your secret," Heath said like a challenge. "I'm not the shameful, failed reed master to be hidden under a pile of goat dung."

"That wasn't me, you know that."

"I know that," Heath said softly. "Miss me all you like," started to say. Ash looked stricken, like he might throw up. Heath took a moment, folding his thoughts in upon itself. "This has to be more like clan leader to clan leader, Calatheas to Melaleuca."

"Many pacts, bonds, and agreements are ratified through marriage."

"No," stepping back. "You know that's right out."

"Let's not be hasty," said in a rush. "There's plenty of time to discuss . . . negotiate."

"Clan leader to clan leader."

"Pacts and bonds—"

"Clan leader to clan leader," interrupting.

Ash drew breath, catching words in his throat, mustering thoughts, and then he stood tall, as if he had reached a decision.

"Clan Calatheas," Ash said, extending his hand.

"Clan Melaleuca," Heath replied, accepting Ash's hand.

The handshake was formal, quiet.

Ash turned, left the backstage area. Heath held still, feeling the breath in his heart, letting it flow slowly from his chest. Chardonnay returned.

"Hey," Chardonnay said by way of asking how he was doing.

"I'm . . . fine," Heath replied, meaning things—thoughts and feelings—were much more complex than he could describe.

"Okay," reaching out.

Heath took Chardonnay's hand. "Okay," he said.

"Sounds like Peregrine hasn't started any fights yet,"

motioning toward the audience barely concealed by the backstage area.

"The night's young," Heath said.

"I suppose we should—" meaning they should join Peregrine and the crowd, but moving close, drawing Heath into his arms.

"There's time," Heath said.

"The night's young."

"The night—as they say—is young."

They didn't quite have privacy, but it was enough.

Gallery

There are fewer representations of the fire-breathing goats of death in art than one might think, considering the out-sized role they have played throughout human history. Quite simply, the goats dislike "graven images" being made of them. This is not something they have told us—the goats do not talk, after all—but it is something they have made abundantly clear through their actions.

For example, they seem to know when a photograph has been taken of them and will do everything in their power to murder the person, destroy the camera, and burn anyone and anything in the general vicinity to cinders.

Less realistic work is the artist's best hope of surviving the attempt to depict them. Anonymity is also the artist's friend, or at least, makes it harder to learn the artist's gruesome fate.

Following are some of the more notoriously well-known pieces.

Goat Net

The Goat Net is one of the more famous recent paintings not only because we know the name of the artist, Kusama, but more importantly, because she survived the experience. The same cannot be said for galleries that have displayed it. Three of them have burned to the ground, and a fourth fell over.

The first gallery, *Soapstone*, burned more than a month after the painting had been purchased, leaving the connection a superstitious coincidence until the painting's owner was eventually found boiled alive in her own swimming pool.

The second gallery, *Victorious Flirtation*, spontaneously burst into flame during the opening-night gala. There were no survivors.

A fifth gallery, *Pennystreet*, did not burn. This upset the gallery owners so much they tried to set fire to it themselves. They failed, dying in the attempt. The attempted arson was discovered when a smell was detected, firefighters were dispatched, and the owners' bodies were found, having suffocated on the gasoline and turpentine fumes.

Goat Net remains in active demand at galleries throughout the world where thrill-seeking patrons bet on whether they will survive the experience.

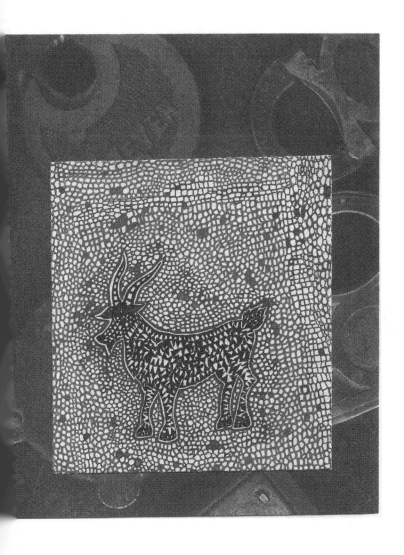

Goat Mosaic Fragment

Little is known of the origins and history of the *Goat Mosaic Fragment*. It is one of the few surviving pieces of a great work depicting the legendary and much disputed tale of the fire-breathing goats of death stampede across Crete. It may have been a migration. Details are sketchy.

The fragments were uncovered by the archaeological team of Winegard and Janet during a freak solar eclipse that was said to have been so complete that not even torches or flashlights could pierce the dark. Winegard claimed the mosaic itself glowed, leading them to it. The experience left him with nightmares that eventually drove him to a deeply passionate love of musical theater. He abandoned archaeology.

Janet was heartbroken. She claimed ownership of the fragments, disputing that Winegard was even at the archaeological site that day. She wrote a well-researched and scholarly account of the experience, history of the archaeological site, and theories surrounding the mosaic.

Winegard wrote the book for an experimental musical comedy. It was never produced.

Hellenic Plate

Depictions of the fire-breathing goats of death are greatly prized not only because of their rarity but also because of the inherent risk in possessing them. Kings, despots, and warlords display them proudly, laughing in the face of danger, bragging of the rivers of blood waded through to acquire them.

The original *Hellenic Plate* made its way into the hands of Menelaus, King of Sparta. He displayed it proudly, as was to be expected, and bragged about it endlessly, boring dinner guests to tears. Priam, King of Troy, coveted the plate and sent his son Paris to acquire it. Paris seduced Menelaus' wife, Helen, convincing her to leave her husband, return with him to Troy, and most importantly, bring the plate.

Learning of his wife's "abduction," Menelaus was said to have been indifferent and wholly unconcerned, stating that he never liked her anyway. Learning she had taken the prized *Hellenic Plate* with her, Menelaus was enraged, declaring the theft to be an act of war.

The campaign to recover the *Hellenic Plate* lasted ten years, consumed two empires, and ended with the city of Troy burned to the ground.

The *Hellenic Plate* was thought lost to history and little more than an apocryphal tale told by a blind-drunk storyteller. It was eventually uncovered in the ruins of Pompeii, confirming its existence. The plate's proximity to a famous and spectacularly destructive volcanic eruption surprised absolutely no one.

German Tournament Shield

The *German Tournament Shield* was said to be the prized possession of Baron Friedrich von Munchausen. He claimed to have discovered it at auction, covered in cobwebs and dust, and had been drawn to it by the outrageously gaudy layers of paint that had been slathered over it. At auction, the shield depicted two drunken sailors and a disgusted cat. Cleaning the dust and cobwebs, Baron von Munchausen had uncovered the extent of alterations, and eventually, the original fire-breathing goats of death beneath.

Baron von Munchausen became obsessed with the history of the shield, traipsing all over the countryside with it in a wagon, holding the shield up to people, and asking if anyone recognized it. He learned the *Tournament Shield* was feared, spreading grief, famine, war, and madness. The alterations and layers of paint had been attempts to deprive the shield of its power.

Growing wary of the cursed history of the shield, Baron von Munchausen considered abandoning it in a ditch. He found a pot of gold in the ditch and a rather fetching young woman who said she would love him forever if only he took the gold, the shield, and the wagon home with him. They were happily married for over thirty years.

Baron von Munchausen said his only regret was that his young bride—whose name he never learned—would bite the heads off servants and drink their blood. This was believed to be an exaggeration. She probably ripped their throats out.

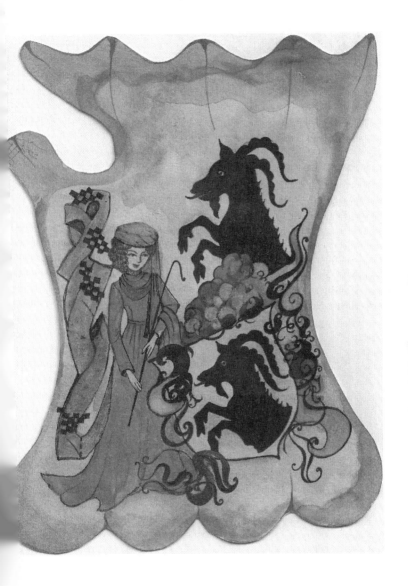

Egyptian Tomb Painting

Little is known of the origins of the fire-breathing goats of death, how long they have been around, or why they have not wiped out the human race. They could do it, too. Everyone knows they could, even if they refuse to accept the truth.

Works like the *Egyptian Tomb Painting* are given as evidence that the goats have not always been so antagonistic toward humanity. There may have even been a time when man and fire-breathing goat lived together in peace and harmony.

Philosophers such as Marks and Edgewise hypothesized that the industrial revolution and general dehumanization of man led the goats to the conclusion that humanity deserved to die. This did not go over well with the bourgeoisie and assorted ruling classes.

Edgewise was stoned to death, his body burned in the public square. Marks fled in horror, changed his name—a little—and continued to write about capitalism and the violence inherent in the system.

Medieval Manuscript

Stories continued to flourish about the history and origins of the fire-breathing goats of death. The vast majority of these tales remained strictly part of the western oral tradition, for fear the goats would take unnatural justice against any who wrote the stories down. There was a push by St. Francis Robin Drake during the Middle Ages to commit some of the tales to manuscript. St. Francis was alternately described as brave and foolhardy by anyone who knew him usually while running quickly in the other direction.

The most infamous result of St. Francis' attempts to bind the stories to the written word was *The Heliotropic Eulogy*, a far-ranging tome that described the fire-breathing goats in such a way that it was easy to imagine the work was describing something else. This obfuscation was probably what saved people's lives. *The Apollonian Bestiary*, another of St. Francis' attempts to describe the goats, was known to blind people who so much as looked at it. Touching the *Bestiary* would cause the person's fingers to burn instantly right down to the bone.

The *Medieval Manuscript* page is from *The Heliotropic Eulogy* and depicts Gilgamesh dancing with one of his goats. Scholars theorize this was an attempt to show a connection between the fire-breathing goats of death and the dancing men. Scholars would typically hazard such theories while running very fast the other way.

Ghost Plate

The fame and notoriety of the *Ghost Plate* started early, beginning with the fact the plate remains unfinished to this day. It started life as a simple tin-plate advertisement for cigarettes. The artist—anonymous for his safety—went to work on it one day and found the goat staring out at him. Shocked and terrified, the artist covered the plate, tried to hide it, but he heard the goat call out to him.

Slowly, over weeks and months, the artist began showing the plate to friends and fellow arts. They swore the goat seemed incredibly lifelike and followed them around the room, turning its head, but nobody ever actually saw it move. All agreed the goat seemed curious about the world, as if it had found a window and wanted to gaze at everyone and everything that it could see.

Rumors and tales of the *Ghost Plate* spread like wildfire through the artistic community, and people longed to see it. They hounded the artist, offered him gifts, attempted to bribe him for just a glimpse of the infamous plate, but this only seemed to drive the artist deeper into madness and despair. At last, he hid the *Ghost Plate* and swore that none would ever see it again.

Prince Francisco Adelaide de Mise-en-scene wanted the *Ghost Plate* more than anything else he had ever desired in his life. He hired detectives. He made rash donations to museums, established *The Franciscan Foundation for the Preservation of the Arts*, and placed outrageous bids on horrid art that nobody else could

possibly want. He did all of this in the hopes of drawing the artist of the *Ghost Plate* out of hiding.

The artist, sending Prince Francisco a note, promised to display the *Ghost Plate*. Prince Francisco arranged a lavish reception, bought the opera house, stating it was the only building in the entire city grand enough for the occasion, and invited more people than even the opera house could hold.

At last—at long last—the *Ghost Plate* was ready, covered by a simple cloth on the stage. The auditorium was full, every seat taken. The black market for tickets had risen into the tens of thousands.

People waited, breaths hushed, as Prince Francisco crossed the stage. The artist had given the prince the honor of revealing the simple, unfinished tin-plate advertisement for cigarettes. Prince Francisco uncovered the *Ghost Plate* with a flourish, and the audience gasped with a shocked inrush of breath and soul-searing cry of despair.

The goat was gone.

The *Ghost Plate* still exists. It is in the hands of a private collector who was once friends with Prince Francisco. The private collector will even show you the *Ghost Plate*, if you know the right people and you know how to ask. The goat may even look back at you as you look at it. The goat—it would seem—remains curious about the world.

The Goat's Sabbath

Nell the Younger was obsessed with the story that a fire-breathing goat of death had once learned to talk. It was said the goat would carry on at great length, teaching, debating, and entertaining crowds. The story consumed Nell the Younger so much that she commis-

sioned a painting. The artist—whose name was never discovered despite all the surrounding accounts—didn't know what to think. The more Nell the Younger tried to explain, the more deranged she sounded.

The artist eventually went off to fulfill the commission, vanishing for seven years. It is said the artist created draft after draft, painting after painting, declaring each one to be imperfect or incomplete. Stories abounded that more than one draft spontaneously burst into flames.

The artist appeared unannounced on Nell the Younger's doorstep one night looking a fright, torn clothes, blackened teeth, blood dripping from rotten fingernails. Staying only long enough to confirm Nell the Younger was home, the artist ran away, screaming, crying, never to be seen again. The painting was found leaning against the doorstep. Nell the Younger was too scared to touch it, leaving it where it had appeared for seven days. During that time, nobody would approach the house. Dogs would howl. Children would cry. Women would swoon.

At last, Nell the Younger took the painting into the great hall, uncovering it for the first time, admiring it, and then promptly died. Her body has never been moved. Servants would become unnaturally terrified and violently ill, approaching or attempting to move her body. It was almost as if the painting enjoyed looking down at the slowly rotting corpse of the person who had commissioned it.

The painting was mounted on the wall in the great hall where it would have a clear view of Nell the Younger's corpse. Nobody knows why. The painting remains in the great hall to this very day and can be viewed if you can stomach the smell.

Tunisian Cave Painting

The quickest way to start a fight among historians, scientists, and fire-breathing goat of death enthusiasts is to ask when the goats first appeared. Some would point to the *Tunisian Cave Painting* as evidence the goats have been around for an exceptionally long time. Others would insist to their dying breath that the cave painting depicts normal, boring, everyday goats.

When Dr. Reginald Vainglory presented his famous paper that the *Tunisian Cave Painting* depicted the goats being granted dominion over fire, the ensuing riot lasted days. Fires were started—blamed on the goats, of course—and Dr. Vainglory was garroted with the conference lanyard belonging to Dr. Susan Eldritch Horror. She denied having murdered him. The conference ended rather abruptly.

Learning to Fly

The fire-breathing goats of death once tried to learn to fly. They would climb trees and leap from the highest branches, usually landing on their heads. Cats, they were not. Birds, they were not.

The goats abandoned this pastime at some point from embarrassment or from having grown tired of roasting anyone and everyone who saw them fall. Details are unclear.

Stories persist, people claiming they saw the fire-breathing goats hanging out in trees. They are goats. They climb. Nobody should find this unusual except it is so rare to catch the goats in trees. When goats are found, it typically turns out to have been perfectly normal ordinary goats, not their fire-breathing brethren.

The title of the painting, *Learning to Fly*, and the fact the goats depicted could be nothing more than ordinary goats is probably what saved the artist's life. The artist, Rackham, knew he was playing with fire when

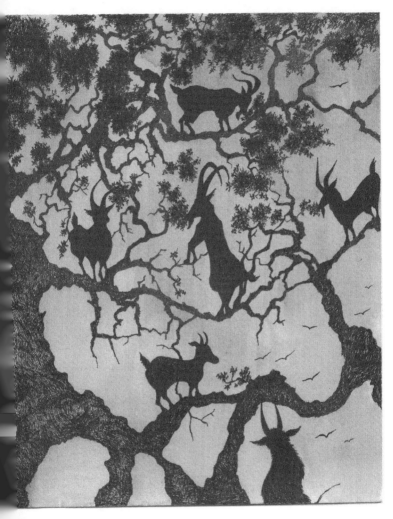

he started work on the painting. He went so far as to prepare his will and say goodbye to his family before starting.

Galleries and art collectors were downright disappointed when nothing bad happened to him. The near miss with the enraged hippopotamus was written off as an unrelated coincidence, although there was speculation about the Komodo dragon that tried to eat his foot. Nobody could figure out how the great big honking lizard had gotten into his bathtub or remained undiscovered for the three days nobody had gone into the bathroom, so speculation dwindled. People lost interest.

The painting remains a favorite in active rotation at galleries, hoping something interesting or eventful will happen.

Afterword

The Urban Goatherds is a pandemic baby and poor homage to the fake commercials for self-published supernatural romance novelist D'Ancey LaGuarde that would appear throughout the run of Alice Fraser's podcast *The Last Post*. There are no half-vampire/half-leprechaun detectives or half-werewolf/half-granddaughters to be found among the urban goatherds, nor are there any amnesiac princesses who know they are being hunted but cannot remember why. I think she was a princess. The exact wording escapes me, and I wasn't able to find it on the List of D'Ancey LaGuarde novels at The Bugle Wiki when I looked. I could look again, but I am exhausted and cannot be bothered. Life is short. Google it, if you want, and you will find the list.

I'm drifting.

I should try to explain.

The first year of the pandemic was rough, and it was rough for reasons that had very, very little to do with COVID. I am not going into detail but trust me when I say things were not good. It was hard to find anything good, and one thing that did—one thing I looked forward to every morning—was a podcast called *The Last Post*.

The podcast was wonderful. It was silly. It leaned into the pandemic, which the podcast had no way of knowing was going to strike right when the show started, and details would occasionally creep into the show about everything the real Alice Fraser was dealing with. She was not having a fun time, to put it mildly.

The Last Post existed in an alternate universe very

much like our own, but ever so slightly different. A sentient trash island running for President of the United States was one of those differences, and the Wiggles running Italy because of babies accidentally voting was another. Tentacle time was never explained, and Neil Gaiman barely escaped from the wicker man on Summerisle. Yes, Neil Gaiman was on *The Last Post*. It was really him performing the role of alternate-universe Neil Gaiman.

There were commercials for half a glass of water, and most importantly, there were commercials for a self-published supernatural romance novelist. I found myself looking forward to the D'Ancey LaGuarde commercials and being delighted when one would appear. The commercials were wonderful, and the summaries of each novel were insane. Half-vampires and half-werewolves were among the many supernatural twists.

The pandemic had played silly buggers with my creative energies, and I knew—I just knew—that I wasn't going to get anywhere with the further adventures of my hardscrabble journalist/underappreciated magician Allison Merriweather. The second Merriweather novel was all mapped out and ready to go when the plague years struck. The timing sucked. Merriweather's future exploits went on indefinite hold.

As the first year of the pandemic dragged, I wanted to do something—anything—to boost my spirits and try to be creative, so I decided to write a D'Ancey LaGuarde inspired supernatural-romance-novel summary, and it was glorious. It was also really juvenile and embarrassing, and it will hopefully never see the light of day.

There was a lot more masturbation and bestiality than made it into the final novella, and the goats were just goats. That was the first big change once I decided

I would try to expand the summary. The story wasn't supernatural enough, so the goats became fire-breathing goats, and a great big heaping pile of story quickly followed after.

The Urban Goatherds was meant to be silly. It was meant to be stupid, but I'm not a romance-novel aficionado. I didn't know the tropes, so I didn't feel comfortable satirizing them. I feared it would come across as condescending and cruel, so I knew the attempts at romance and the relationships had to be sincere. The characters would have silly names, and the world they inhabited would be very silly. There were fire-breathing goats of death, for one thing, and the goatherds would spend most of their time dealing with the dung.

Many of the details survived from the original summary, like the orgies, the rival clans, and the goat trials, but I knew I had to let the story go where it would rather than force it to be something it was not. The final novella is nowhere near as funny, crazy, supernatural, or smutty as any of the D'Ancey LaGuarde summaries. I did the best I could.

The Urban Goatherds owes everything to Alice Fraser and *The Last Post* podcast. If you have found anything worthwhile in this story, please seek out Alice Fraser's work. She has two active podcasts at the time of writing this afterword—*Tea With Alice*, and *The Gargle*. She has multiple stand-up comedy specials available via Amazon, and she can be supported via Patreon.

It's worth your bother to investigate.

Made in the USA
Columbia, SC
11 July 2024

38260775R00091